W9-AQJ-787

The

Ghost
Soldiers

An Imprint of HarperCollins*Publishers*

The
Ghost
Soldiers

POEMS

James Tate

HarperCollins books may be purchased for educational, business, or sales promotional use. For information, please write: Special Markets Department, HarperCollins Publishers, 10 East 53rd Street, New York, NY 10022.

FIRST EDITION

Designed by Sunil Manchikanti

Library of Congress Cataloging-in-Publication Data
Tate, James, 1943–
   The ghost soldiers : poems / by James Tate. — 1st ed.
    p. cm.
   ISBN: 978-0-06-143694-9
   I. Title.
   PS3570.A8G48 2008
   811'.54—dc22

                            2007029856

08 09 10 11 12   ID/RRD   10 9 8 7 6 5 4 3 2 1

For Dara,
for Emily
and Guy

Acknowledgments

Agni Review, Crazyhorse, The Gettysburg Review, Hollins Critic, Hunger Mountain, The Mississippi Review, New American Writing, The New Yorker, The Paris Review, and *Tin House*

Contents

"The paratroopers fall and as they fall
They mow the lawn."

Wallace Stevens

The
Ghost
Soldiers

TREASON

The man that was following me looked like a government agent, so I turned around and walked up to him and said, "Why are you following me?" He said, "I'm not following you. I'm an insurance agent walking to work." "Well, pardon me, my mistake," I said. "Have you done something wrong, unpatriotic, or are you just paranoid?" he said. "I've done nothing wrong, certainly not unpatriotic, and I'm not paranoid," I said. "Well, nobody's ever mistaken me for a government agent before," he said. "I'm sorry," I said. "You have something weighing down on your conscience, don't you?" he said. "No, I don't. I'm just vigilant," I said. "Like a good criminal," he said. "Would you stop talking to me like that," I said. "I don't want to have anything to do with you." "You've committed some kind of treason and they're going to get you," he said. "You're out of your mind," I said. "Benedict Arnold, that's who you are," he said. "I'm going to a peace rally if that's okay with you," I said. "Oh, a peacenik. That's the same as treason," he said. "No, it isn't," I said. "Yes it is," he said. "No." "Yes." "No." "Yes." We reached his office door. "I really hate to say good-bye to you. Would you like to have lunch tomorrow?" he said. "I'd be delighted," I said. "Good. Then Sadie's Café at noon," he said. "Noon at Sadie's," I said.

I reached out my hand in one direction and felt something like silk, a silk scarf fit for a princess. I reached out my other hand and something bit it, a monkey perhaps. Thus, I concluded, I must be in India. Someone entered the room and said, "Get up!" I attempted to stand but was bent double. I attempted to straighten out, but I could not. "Stand up straight," the voice said. "Sir, I cannot. This is how I am shaped," I said. "All right, march over here," he said. I had only a vague idea of where he was, but I marched over there, if you could call that marching. "Stop," he said, and I stopped. "You are to meet the captain and he is a very important man. You must listen to him and follow out his orders. Do you understand?" he said. "Oh, yes, sir, I will do exactly as I am ordered," I said. He opened a door and then another door and then another door. And then, finally, there was the captain bent over his desk with a green light shining on him. I was still bent over to my waist, but, still, I waited for him to notice me. He said nothing. I started singing a little ditty beneath my breath. Finally, he looked up and said, "What are you, some kind of crippled rabbit or something?" "That's very funny, sir. Crippled rabbit I may be, but I am here to follow your orders," I said. "That's my boy. Now can you hop for me," he said. I concentrated all my efforts and started to hop around the room. "Excellent," he said. "Now can you bend over further and sneak around the room as quietly as you can," he said. The captain was just a green blur to me. I couldn't really see him. Still, I did what I was told, nearly bumping into a chair I didn't see. "Now I want you to charge me with all your might and see if you can knock me over," he said. "Sir, I weigh only a few pounds and am quite sickly. I do not think this is a fair contest," I said.

"Who said anything about fair? I intend to crush you into a little ball of fur," he said. He really did think I was a rabbit. This bothered me. After so many years in the infirmary, how could anybody think I was still a rabbit. I slunk out of his room with my head nearly banging against my knees, longing for my bed again, not knowing if I'd ever find it.

I asked Jasper if he had any ideas about the coming revolution. "I didn't know there was a revolution coming," he said. "Well, people are pretty disgusted. There might be," I said. "I wish you wouldn't just make things up. You're always trying to fool with me," he said. "There are soldiers everywhere. It's hard to tell which side they're on," I said. "They're against us. Everyone's against us. Isn't that what you believe?" he said. "Not everyone. There are a few misguided stragglers who still believe in something or other," I said. "Well, that gives me heart," he said. "Never give up the faith," I said. "Who said I ever had any?" he said. "Shame on you, Jasper. It's important to believe in the cause," I said. "The cause of you digging us deeper into a hole?" he said. "No, the cause of the people standing together for their rights, freedom and all," I said. "Well, that's long gone. We have no rights," he said. We fell silent for the next few minutes. I was staring out the window at a rabbit in the yard. Finally, I said, "I was just saying all that to amuse you." "So was I," he said. "Do you believe in God?" I said. "God's in prison," he said. "What'd he do?" I said. "Everything," he said.

THE MEMORY PALACE

There wasn't a light on in the place at that time of night.
I walked around in back and tried the door. Of course it was
locked. There was a thick vine growing up the side of the building,
so I tried climbing that. I was almost up when it started to
wobble and detach itself from the building. I came crashing
down and cut my forehead and arms. I found a fire escape in front
and climbed that. I broke into the second-story window and was
amazed to find stacks and stacks of photo albums and files overflowing
on the floor. I turned on a light, though I knew the dangers of
that. There seemed to be no order to anything. I pulled up a
chair and picked up an album—children on ponies in cowboy outfits,
children holding fish they caught, birthday cakes, parties,
swings, dances, no end to the fascination with children, but
somehow they all seemed to be a part of the same childhood. Then
there was the album of the near-dead, breathing tubes, feeding
bags, the glazed, faraway looks of the nearly departed. In
the Memory Palace nothing is lost, just misplaced. I spent most
of the night there until I was so exhausted I could barely keep
my eyes open. While going through the many albums devoted to
young lovers, I suddenly froze. There was a photo of my mother
and father, badly faded, barely twenty years old, perhaps not
even married yet, holding hands and smiling into the camera,
the world holding back its fury for one brief second, giving

them their moment of sunshine, so fragile and tenuous. I removed the photo from its pocket and stuck it in mine. I went to the window and looked down. An old man in a uniform stood there. "Come on down, son, we're going to have to arrest you," he said. "But, officer, I'm an old man," I said. "The Memory Palace has no memory. See, it just doesn't care," he said.

PLAN B

Joaquin said to forget the old plan. It had been thoroughly replaced with a new plan. "Okay, what's the new plan?" I said. "Some final details have to be worked out, but we'll have it soon," he said. "So, we are between plans, which means, at the moment, we don't have a plan," I said. "I wouldn't put it like that. That's putting a negative spin on our otherwise bright future," he said. "I'll wait for the revised plan before I start talking about our bright future," I said. "We're just in a crevasse right now, hunkering down, keeping watch," he said. "I feel like I'm lost and vulnerable, without a map, ready to be taken out with the first volley," I said. Darrell walked into the room just then. "What's wrong with you?" he said. "I'm lost," I said. "Well, I've seen the second plan and it's much better than the first, trust me," he said. "But when will it arrive?" I said. "Soon, they're almost finished with it, just a few finishing touches," he said. Joaquin said, "These guys really know what they're doing, they're the best." "I don't even know who they are," I said. "You're not supposed to," Darrell said. "It's none of your business," Joaquin said. "But I'm not some kind of laboratory rat," I said. "You'll be all right, you'll see," Darrell said. A little later a man with a mask on came in and handed Joaquin a piece of paper. After the man left, Joaquin said, "Okay, follow me." We went out on the street and started walking. A man said hello to me and I said hello back. "Was that okay, Joaquin?" I said. "Very good," he said. A while later a girl I knew came up and hugged me. "Joaquin, was that a mistake?" I said. "No, perfect," he said. Finally, we went into the ice-cream parlor. A waitress took our order. A woman came up to Darrell and said, "Mind if I join you?" Darrell said, "Of course not, please do." She said, "Darrell, I've missed you. Where have you been?" Darrell looked at Joaquin, Joaquin nodded. Then Darrell said, "Plan B has allowed me to find you. We must always be grateful for that." "Glory be to Plan B," we all spoke together. I started licking my chocolate cone with a deep sense of mystery.

A red Frisbee sailed overhead and we all knelt down
and prayed. What we were praying for I don't know. In fact,
I didn't even know what I was doing with this group of lunatics.
They were constantly looking for signs. I didn't really
believe in that kind of thing. But when they kneeled to pray,
I did too, only I didn't really pray. "What do you think that
flock of pigeons means?" one of them said to me. "It means
we have strayed from God's embrace," I said. "Tragic,
isn't it?" he said. "Indeed," I said. We walked on through
a field of clover. There was an old tractor covered with rust.
One woman stumbled and fell. "Leave her. She will be a hindrance
to us," the leader said. Two deer saw us and started to run.
"O holy days, the end is near," my companion said. We all fell
down and started to pray. "I don't think the end is near,"
someone said. "Of course the end is near," someone else said.
"Two deer running away, that's the sign, isn't it?" "Two deer
running away means something wonderful is about to happen," I
said. "I didn't see any deer. I think you just imagined them,"
someone said. "We had better be moving on. It's going to get
dark soon," the leader said. Soon, we entered a forest. "I think
this is a mistake. We're going to get lost," I said. "Lost is
for the unbeliever. There will be a sign, mark my word," he
said. "The forest has too many signs," I said. A pileated

woodpecker swooped down and flew right over us. "This is where we are meant to camp," the leader said. It was dusk when we set up the tents. "I don't like it here," I said. "God won't let us down. He never does," my companion said. Night fell. I said, "We must get out of here. Something terrible is going to happen to us." There was no answer. So, with my flashlight on, I started walking through the trees. I never did like those people. They were a lost tribe, and I wasn't lost, just confused.

THE NEW HORSES

When the horses arrived I was so happy. I put them out
in the field and they seemed to like it, except for the flies.
Then, later, I made sure they got fed. The pinto bucked up
and kicked the fence, which shocked me, but then everything
was all right again. Later, when they settled down for the night,
there was a sound like a snake hissing in one of the stalls,
but I couldn't find anything. In the morning, when I let them
out, the bay was limping. I tried to examine her, but she kicked
me in the head and I was out for a good fifteen minutes before
I woke. She was all right by then. The sorrel had jumped the fence
while I was out and I went and got the truck. I found her about
three miles down the road. Someone in a truck or car had grazed
her and she was lying down by the side of the road. I managed
to pull her up and she made it up the plank into the back of
the truck. When I let her back in the pen, I realized her leg
was broken and she would have to be shot. The chestnut let out
a loud whinny. The roan walked over and stomped on my foot very
deliberately. My foot hurt, but, more importantly, my feelings
were hurt. I really wanted to make these horses happy. The pinto
took off running and crashed into the fence. The chestnut started
chasing the sorrel until the sorrel collapsed. My head was buzzing,
my stomach churning. The bay jumped over the tractor and was
headed right for me. I ran out of the pen and shut the fence.

The sorrel was suffering. I had to put her out of her misery. I got my rifle from the house. I loved these horses, I really did, but something wasn't right with them. The chestnut wouldn't let me in the gate. The pinto started chanting in Latin. The roan looked like it had grown a horn in its forehead. I started firing every which way, blind as a bat.

THE NATIVE AMERICANS

"We found them on your lawn this morning, about seventy-five of them," the officer said. "What are they?" I said. "Well, they're some kind of Native Americans, we don't know what kind yet, but we will. We used an electrical device to paralyze them, but they'll start coming to in about twenty-four hours. Some of them will only live for about an hour, and others could live as long as sixty years. So we'll start in reeducating them right away," he said. "But where did they come from?" I said. "Well, we don't really know, but some of our scientists think they just rose up out of the ground, some signal goes off in them, like a timer," he said. "You mean all this time I have been living in a cemetery?" I said. "Apparently," he said. "Well, that explains a lot," I said. "What do you mean?" he said. "Just recently I have felt the house shake a lot at night, and I thought I heard distant cries, and I would wake covered in sweat, which I thought was blood," I said. "Why don't you come down here tomorrow morning and we'll show you some of the men," he said. "Thank you, officer," I said. Of course I was made miserable by the thought that these men had been buried beneath my lawn all these years, but what could I do? The lawn was an unholy mess. It would have to be completely redone in the spring. I showed up at the police department around 10:00 the next morning as told. There behind glass doors were these half-awake men, moaning and shuffling about. "They don't look very dangerous," I said to the officer. "That's why I wanted you to come in early. I didn't want you to see that part of it," he said.

"What do you do then?" I said. "More electricity. Then slowly we start to reeducate. Some of them will go quite far," he said.

"And what about the others?" I said. "Oh, we'll rebury them with a jolt that will keep them down a good long time," he said. "In my yard?" I said. "That's their native ground," he said.

TWO VISIONS

"I look around and I see two figures running across a landscape, their coats in tatters, their legs about to give out," I said. "That's funny. I see two figures dancing around a swing, flowers in their hair, a song bursting from their lips," Nikki said. "They are falling down and crawling. I think, perhaps, they are dying of thirst," I said. "These people are in love. It is so obvious. They can't keep their hands off one another," she said. "Wait a minute. There's a third man on a horse. He rides up to them, offers them a drink from his canteen. He dismounts and offers them the horse. He helps them up and leads the horse," I said. "She slaps him. He has said something terribly wrong. He raises his hand," she said. "Nikki," I said, "why aren't we looking at the same picture?" "But we are, Harvey. It's the same picture, it's just that you have some funny ideas of your own," she said. "I'm just reporting what I see," I said. "Well, go on then," she said. "These men on camels arrive and surround them. There must be thirty of them carrying sabers," I said. "The lovers have embraced and are kissing," she said. "Your people are so predictable," I said. "I'm sorry. What am I supposed to do about it?" she said. "It's not your fault. I guess there's nothing you can do," I said. "The Chieftain gets down from his camel and points his saber at the man leading the horse. He's demanding money to cross the desert." "I'm so

worried about your people. I don't think they're going to get
out of there alive," she said. "What about your people?" I said.
"I can't see them. They're nowhere around," she said. "Maybe
they're dead in the gutter. Did you check the gutters?" I said.
"I've checked everywhere. She left her scarf on the swing,"
she said. "Probably just went for some ice cream. She'll be
back," I said. "What about yours?" she said. "You don't want
to know. I'm sorry I ever tied up with them. They never had
a chance from the beginning," I said. "But they were your kind
of people. You liked them," she said. We sat there staring out
into space for quite a while. Finally, I said, "What about your
people?" She said, "What about them?" I said, "Did you kill
them?" "I don't want to talk about that now. It's such a beautiful
night."

NOTHING IS WHAT IT SEEMS

"Nothing is what it seems." Morgan had said this to me
the other day. It sounded profound, but I doubted the true
wisdom of it. I mean, I know there is a lot of illusion in
the world, but the shoe store is still the shoe store, my razor
is just a razor, my hat is a hat. Morgan had probably been reading
a Zen book. He's like that, goes off on these weird jags and
comes spouting off to me. I don't mind it. It gives me some-
thing to think about. Once he told me that ghosts were real,
and that I shouldn't be afraid of them because they are terribly
lonely and just want company. I said I had never seen a ghost,
and he said I wasn't looking in the right way. He never told
me what the right way was. I suspect it involves a spectroflu-
orometer, and I don't have one. But neither does Morgan. I like
to sit out and watch the stars at night. There are billions in
the Milky Way. Of course we can only see a few thousand, and that is
plenty for me. Every now and then one of them falls, out of
hydrogen after twenty-five billion years or more. I often wonder
where they are going at such tremendous speed. Our sun's
going to go out in twenty-five billion years, what then?

"HONEY, CAN YOU HEAR ME?"

Alison stared into the mirror and combed her hair. How beautiful she was! "I look awful," she said. I bent down and tied my shoe and hit my head on the coffee table on the way up. "Ouch," I said. "What did you say, honey?" she said. "I said we ought to buy a new couch," I said. "I thought we just bought one," she said. "We could buy another one so we'd have a backup in case anything happens to this one," I said. She didn't answer me, but continued to brush her hair. I stared down at my shoes and said, "Something is so wrong there." "What did you say, honey?" she said. I said, "It will be wonderful to be there tonight." "Where's that, honey?" she said. "Wherever it is that we're going," I said. "We're not going anywhere," she said. "I meant here. It will be wonderful to be here tonight," I said. "A little romantic night at home," she said. What did she mean by "nomadic"? A little nomadic night at home. There were times when I worried about Alison. She hovered right on the borderline, about to cross over into her own private realm, where nothing she sees or hears corresponds to anything in the known world. I live with this fear daily. My shoes are on the wrong feet, or so it seems to me now.

A BOY AND HIS COW

I sat on my couch and hummed a little tune. I didn't recognize it, but, still, I continued to hum. I was going into a trance and felt dizzy. I leapt up and said, "This is not a good idea, boy. Snap out of it. You have responsibilities, places to go, things to see, people to meet, worlds to conquer." Then I fell to the floor and lay there with one eye open, twitching. I had been attacked by a brutal imp. I was having trouble moving my limbs. I said, "You'll be sorry for this." A hand reached down and pulled me up, a hand belonging to no one. I got myself a glass of water and drank it. It started leaking out of me. I went and called the plumber. "I've got leaks," I said. I was hoping I could save the day, because I had great plans, things I had always wanted to do, but never got done. Something was crawling up the wall. It was a Six-Spotted Green Tiger Beetle. That must mean something. Good fortune? Death? I grabbed the glass and quickly captured him and threw him outside. Too risky. I returned to the couch and started to hum a little tune my mother used to sing to me when I was a child about a boy and his cow. And so the afternoon passed into evening, and in the evening I sewed a button on my shirt, and felt really good about that.

I had lots of duct tape, but I never used it. I bought
more just in case. I thought sure an occasion would arise.
I kept looking around. I said to Tracy, "Would you mind if
I covered you in duct tape?" "Just a little bit on the wrist,"
she said. "Thank you," I said. I felt much better. "There's
no telling what's going to happen next," she said. "What do you
mean?" I said. "A satellite fell on the Episcopal Church," she
said. "That's unfortunate," I said. "Was anybody hurt?" "Mrs.
Graves was there. She thinks it was heaven-sent. She was sneaking
a cracker at the time," she said. I took a piece of tape and
stuck it on her back. "Well, I'm just glad she's all right," I
said. "She's psychotic. You know that," she said. I took a
piece of tape and stuck it in her hair. "She's a harmless, old lady
who's afraid of goblins," I said. "She thinks all children are
goblins. She's going to kill one one day," she said. "Andy's
boa constrictor escaped last night," I said. "Who's Andy?" she
said. "He's the manager at Ace's Hardware Store. I thought you
knew him," I said. "Never been to Ace's Hardware Store," she said.
"It's a wonderful place," I said. "What the hell was he doing with
a boa constrictor?" she said. "Kept his house free of pigs,"
I said. "Well, that makes sense," she said. I reached over
and put a piece of tape on her butt. She was looking pretty
good by now.

It wasn't the door I was looking for, but I opened it anyway. I started walking down a long hallway. There was no one in it. There was a series of offices which seemed to be empty. The only noise anywhere was my footsteps. At the farthest end of the hall a man suddenly appeared. He started walking toward me and my instinct told me to run, but I didn't. I stopped and waited for him. When he finally reached me, he said, "We've been waiting for you. You are warmly welcomed." "Thank you," I said, "I am most eager to join you." "Follow me, kind sir," he said. We walked down the long hall. "In here," he said. We entered an office. Twelve men, all formally dressed, stood and gave me an ovation. I bowed to them. "You see," said my guide, "they all love you." "I'm deeply flattered," I said. The truth was I was baffled and certain this was one big mistake. "We want you to become one of us, to become a member of the Holy Alliance. What do you say, will you do it?" he said. All the members were smiling at me. "But I don't really know what the Holy Alliance is," I said. "Well, we believe we have been chosen by God to bring order and justice to the community, and every now and then we have a party," he said. "I need to step outside and think about it," I said. I moved rather quickly to the door and started running down the hallway. I made it to the door and stepped outside. There were crowds of people on the sidewalk and I wove in and out of them as quickly as I could. A man in a wheelchair grabbed my hand as I tried to pass him. "Have you seen my canary? He flew out my window this morning," he said. "No, I haven't seen your canary, but I will keep an eye out for him and try to catch him if I do. I'll bring him back to you, you can count on that," I said. "I knew I could trust you. God bless you," he said. I wrenched my hand free and raced on. A while later, I did spot a canary, but it was perched on the top branch of a tall maple, too far from me. I stared at it and tried to hypnotize it. It was looking right at me. I took a step toward it, then another. A man walked by and grabbed it right off the bush and stuck it in his pocket. "Hey, that's my bird," I said. He was walking fast and didn't even look back at me.

Jack told me to never reveal my true identity. "I would never do that," I said. "Always wear at least a partial disguise," he said. "Of course," I said. "And try to blend in with the crowd," he said. "Naturally," I said. "And never fall in love," he said. "Far too dangerous," I said. "Never raise your voice," he said. "Understood," I said. "Never run," he said. "I wouldn't dream of it," I said. "Never make a glutton of yourself," he said. "It won't happen," I said. "Always be polite," he said. "That's me, polite," I said. "Don't sing in public," he said. "You have my promise," I said. "Don't touch strangers," he said. "That's forbidden," I said. "Never speed," he said. "You can count on me," I said. "Don't wear plaid," he said. "No plaid," I said. "Don't pet dogs," he said. "Of course not," I said. "Don't jump fences," he said. "I won't," I said. "Stay away from children," he said. "I will," I said. "Don't enter churches," he said. "Of course not," I said. "Good posture at all times," he said. "Good posture is a must," I said. "Never pick money out of the gutter," he said. "That's not for me," I said. "Be punctual," he said. "Always on time," I said. "When walking or driving always mix your routes," he said. "Naturally," I said. "Never order the same meal twice," he said. "Never," I said. "Do not be seen on the street after midnight," he said. "Not ever," I said. "Do not give money to homeless beggars," he said. "Nothing for the beggars," I said. "Do not start conversations with officers of the law," he said. "No talking with cops," I said. "No ice skating," he said. "Never," I said. "No skiing," he said. "Of course not," I said. "When a sign says STAY OFF THE GRASS, you'll stay off," he said. "I will," I said. "No chewing gum in public," he said. "I won't," I said. "You must carry your weapon at all times," he said. "Always armed," I said. "You must follow orders," he said. "Count on it," I said. "You will contact Central once a week," he said. "Contact Central," I said. "No green pants," he said. "Certainly not," I said. "No orange or purple shirts," he said. "Not for me," I said. "No sushi," he said. "Oh no," I said. "No fandango," he said. "Not possible," I said. "No farm bureau," he said. "Not my style," I said. "Beware of hypnotism," he said. "Always alert," I said. "Watch out for leeches," he said. "A danger not forgotten," I said. "Stay off gondolas." "Instinctively," I said. "Never trust a fortune-teller," he said. "Never," I said. "Avoid crusades," he said. "Certainly," I said. "Never ride on a blimp," he said. "Blimps are out," I said. "Do not chase turkeys," he said. "I will not," I said. "Do not put your hand in the mouth of a horse," he said. "Out of the question," I said. "Never believe in miracles," he said. "I won't," I said.

ABDUCTED

Mavis claimed to have been abducted by aliens. Maybe she was, I don't know. She said they had intercourse with her, but it was different. They placed a finger in the middle of her forehead and made a buzzing sound. She said it felt better than the other kind of intercourse. I asked her if I could try it and she said no. Not long after that Mavis disappeared for good. She didn't say good-bye to anyone and no one knew where she went. I started dreaming about her. Frequently, they were disturbing dreams, but the ones that involved aliens were very soothing. I think I secretly longed to be abducted. Of course I never confessed this to anyone. I'm not saying I believed Mavis, but I do believe she experienced what she said she did. People see things that aren't there all the time. Some of those people are crazy and some aren't. Mavis wasn't crazy. She wasn't my lover, but we were good friends and I missed her. But life went on. I had a couple of beers with Jared once or twice a week. I went out to dinner or to a movie with Trisha occasionally. Once I knocked on the door of Mavis's old apartment and a woman who spoke no English answered. There was an article in the paper about a woman who had been found at the bottom of a lake. Police had not been able to identify her. I went down to the morgue right away. "I'd like to see the body of the woman who drowned in the lake," I said. "I'm sorry. That's not possible," the man said. "But she may be a friend of mine," I said. "The police have given me strict

orders. No one is to see her," he said. "But I could possibly
identify her," I said. "Trust me, no one could identify what
we have here," he said. I left and returned home. Jared came
over that night. I told him that I was worried that the woman in
the morgue could be Mavis. He said, "Who's Mavis?" I said, "You
know damned well who Mavis is. You had several dates with her.
I think you might have even been falling in love with her, but
she dumped you." "I don't know any Mavis, and I certainly never
dated her. My memory's not that bad," he said. "I saw you at
Donatello's one night with her," I said. "I've never been to
Donatello's," he said. "Jared, why are you doing this?" I said.
"I'm just telling you the truth. I've never known a woman named
Mavis," he said. Later, after Jared left, I started thinking
about it. I couldn't even picture Mavis's face anymore. It
was sad. She was being erased. I wanted to put my finger on
her forehead, but there was nothing there.

THE GOVERNMENT MAN

I ran down the alley and through the parking lot dodging
some cars, then up the hill and down again, alongside the
river as it curved under the bridge, over by the baseball diamond,
behind the church. I climbed the fence and dropped down into
a bed of flowers. I straightened myself and dashed behind the
candy store and over past the liquor store down the little valley
where the statues are. I stopped to catch my breath and look
around. Then I ran into the woods and followed the trail. I
jumped over fallen branches. At some point I frightened three
deer and they took off running. I tripped and almost fell.
I ran until I was breathless. I looked behind me. A man had
tried to pull a net over my head back there, like I was a butter-
fly or something. There was something terribly sinister about
him. I suspect he was a government man from the way he dressed.
It was just a job he had been assigned to do, but I put up a
fight and broke loose. He followed me, of course. I started
running again, crossed a small stream, and up a hill. When I
got to the top, I stopped to look around. I could see nothing
moving in the woods and felt good about that. When I turned
around, the man was standing there with the net, which he slipped
over my head and down past my arms. Then he cinched it with
something. "That's for your own protection," he said. "What
do you mean my protection?" I said. "From yourself. You're

in great danger of hurting yourself," he said. "That's baloney, I am not," I said. "Everybody says that, but we have our ways of knowing," he said. He started pulling me forward on a rope. "You can't treat a human being like this," I said. "You're no longer a human being," he said. "What am I, then?" I said. "You're a soulless beast," he said. "I am not," I said. He yanked the rope harder. I howled in pain.

THE RESTORATIVE

One old lady at the Saturday market will sell you a vial
of weasel urine for thirty-five dollars, which, she says, when
drunk, will reinvigorate your soul. "Where'd you get it?" I
asked her. "I have my sources," she answered. "How do I know
it's not yours?" I said. "Because your soul would not be re-
invigorated if it was mine. Perhaps you are implying that I
am some kind of huckster. Well, I assure you I am not. Weasel urine
has been proven to be an excellent restorative for centuries.
Look around you at all the tired souls. I could help them, but
they laugh at me, sad, weary laughs," she said. "Once, in Texas,
I drank some ghost-faced bat urine," I said. "How'd you get it?"
she asked. "I knew the bat," I said. "Oh," she said. "It was
supposed to give me night vision, but it nearly blinded me for a
month," I said. "You can't be too careful," she said. "But I
can give you a money-back guarantee." "Sounds like a good deal,
but I'll have to think it over," I said. "Suit yourself," she
said. "But I could be sold out in no time." "Oh, all right, I'll
take one," I said. "Just one? You'll be sorry," she said. I
checked my wallet. "Oh, okay, make it three," I said. "I'll
put them in a nice little bag for you. And I'll just stick my
card in there in case you want more. Call me anytime," she said.
Her name was Adela Lea Baider, and I had just given her one hundred
and five dollars for three vials of weasel urine. I already felt

kind of high. I didn't really plan on actually drinking it, but just carrying it around with me in my pocket was awfully exciting. I mingled with the crowds, but I was obviously floating just an inch or two above the ground. I half expected some rough customer to pull me down and slap me for being so imprudent, but that didn't happen. Instead I spotted Hilary buying a bunch of daffodils. Touching her arm, I said, "How are you doing, Hilary?" "Oh, Barney, it's you. I've got a nagging cold. I thought these daffodils might cheer me up. All of us have been sick, so it hasn't been much fun lately. I just had to get out of the house today. We've just been a bunch of zombies," she said. "But, tell me, how have you been?" "Well, right now I'm feeling pretty great, I must admit," I said. "Did you sell a painting at that group show you were in?" she asked. "Well, no, I'm afraid none of the paintings sold, though I had a few nice compliments," I said. "Well, I'm glad you're feeling great. You must give me your secret sometime," she said. Whether she meant that last comment snidely I wasn't sure, but I decided to not share the weasel urine with her. I don't think it would have worked on her. You have to be receptive to it. Perhaps submissive is the better word. I had given myself over to it completely, and was happy to float away from Hilary. The urine was causing my head to spin in the most delightful way. I kept my left hand in my pocket touching the vials as I navigated my way through the crowds. I imagined myself in the throngs of a medieval fair with pipes and drums and grog sloshing in goblets. The mob of bawdy peasants amused me to no end, but I sensed that violence was not far away, and left the scene in favor of my own quiet home. Once there, I placed the vials on the coffee table and stared in wonder. I felt like a very rich man, indeed. No one I know in the whole world has three vials of weasel urine. I could feel my soul tingling. It was white-hot with intoxication. I held one of the vials up to my cheek. And the next second I was in the chicken yard wreaking havoc. And then I slept and was happy.

THE GHOST SOLDIERS

I saw a duck fly into a tree today. Boy, you don't see
that very often. It must have been daydreaming. I was out driving
around, and now that I think of it, it had looked over at me just before
impact. It must have felt so stupid. Anyway, I didn't stop to
see how it was. I wanted to, but I was afraid I would embarrass it.
Just that little glance at me may have done it in. I feel lousy about
it, but it really wasn't my fault. I was on my way to the Memorial
Day parade. Suddenly I wanted to see all these veterans in their
uniforms marching down Main Street. But this duck had flown by
and looked at me, and now its body lay crumpled in a heap. I drove on,
not looking back. The police had cordoned off Main Street, so I had to
turn down a side street and look for a parking place. There were no
parking places for blocks, but eventually I found one. There was a
steady stream of people on the sidewalks, all heading for the parade.
I fell in stride beside them. "It's a nice day for a parade," I said
to one little old lady walking beside me. "You think I'm going to fall
for a tired old line like that? You better think again, mister," she
said. "I was just commenting on the weather," I said. "I didn't mean
to offend you." I kept to myself after that. The parade itself was
rather modest. I counted about thirty-five veterans, ranging in age
from eighty-five to eighteen. Several were in wheelchairs, several
more on crutches, two drummers and one horn player. The crowd just
stared at them in silence. Police patrolled the streets as if the

queen were passing. I looked but saw no queen. The man beside me looked at me and said, "The parade's so small because everyone from this town is always killed. They're just not fit to fight. I don't know why that is. It must be something in the water. They just refuse to shoot. It's odd, isn't it. They've done many studies on it, and they still don't know why it is like that." "Are you trying to pick me up, because, if you are, you're going to have to come up with a better line than that," I said. "What the hell are you talking about?" he said. "I came here to see the queen, but apparently there's no queen," I said. "We got rid of all that royalty crap hundreds of years ago," he said. "Oh," I said, "well, nobody told me." I turned and fought my way through the crowd and walked back to my car. The drive home was uneventful, except that I kept imagining this duck flying beside my car looking at me. It was distracting me, as I was not keeping my eye on the road. One minute it was a soulful, almost loving gaze, and the next it felt accusatory. I narrowly missed an oncoming truck, and the driver honked angrily at me. With that, I bade the duck good-bye and concentrated on driving. It's true, almost no one from this town ever came back from any war. They call them the ghost soldiers, much beloved even by their enemies, and I guess that's why I went to the parade, just to feel them march past, that little rush of cold air.

CRICKET CRICKET

When I am alone on a summer night, and
there is a cricket in the house, I always feel
that things could be worse. Maybe it is raining,
and then thunder and lightning are shaking the
house. The power goes out, and I must grope
around in the darkness for a candle. At last,
the candle is found, but where are the matches?
I always keep them in that drawer. I knock over
a vase, but it doesn't break. Afraid of what
I might break, I return to my chair and sit
there in the darkness. The lightning is striking
all around the house. Then I remember the cricket,
and I listen for its chirping. Soon, the storm
passes, and the lights come back on. An eerie
green silence fills my home. I am worried that
the cricket may have been struck by some light-
ning of its own.

FATHER'S DAY

My daughter has lived overseas for a number
of years now. She married into royalty, and they
won't let her communicate with any of her family or
friends. She lives on birdseed and a few sips
of water. She dreams of me constantly. Her husband,
the Prince, whips her when he catches her dreaming.
Fierce guard dogs won't let her out of their sight.
I hired a detective, but he was killed trying to
rescue her. I have written hundreds of letters
to the State Department. They have written back
saying that they are aware of the situation. I
never saw her dance. I was always away at some
convention. I never saw her sing. I was always
working late. I called her My Princess, to make
up for my shortcomings, and she never forgave me.
Birdseed was her middle name.

Loretta had a rooster that was so fierce
nobody could visit her anymore. Loretta loved
that rooster, and the rooster loved Loretta,
thought she was his wife. So the only time
we got to see Loretta was when she came to town.
We'd meet her at Mike's Westview Café and drink
beer with her all night. The rooster's name
was Waylon, and she'd talk about Waylon all
night, and if you didn't know better you'd think
she was talking about her husband. Well, I knew
better, and I still thought she was talking about
her husband. "Waylon wasn't feeling very good
this morning." "Waylon was real sweet to me
last night." "Waylon is so handsome, sometimes
I just can't take my eyes off him." She's still
fun to be with, and she seems completely normal
to me. At closing time, we say our good-byes,
and I kiss Loretta, just a little peck, because
I know she is married to a chicken, and I respect
that. Waylon has made her happy in ways I never
could. The starry sky, the police hiding in the
bushes, God, it's good to be alive, I think, and
pee behind my car in the darkness of my own private
darkness.

MY CATTLE RANCH

I don't remember much about that particular
evening. Jacqueline insisted on showing me her
navel. She claimed that if I touched it, it
would bring me good luck. I have no idea if I
touched it. Dabney was bragging about his winnings
at the horse track. He said he won nine out of
ten races the week before. I told him I didn't
believe him, and he invited me to go to the track
with him. I told him I wasn't a gambling man,
which was a lie. Beatrice came over and showed
me her navel. It seemed to have a little face
in it, which made me laugh. I asked her if I
could touch it, and she said, "Of course, darling."
I didn't want to stop touching it, but after a
while she needed to go to the ladies' room. Adam
told me about his recent surgery. He showed me
his scar and I dropped my drink. Isabel tried
to sell me some cattle. "Isabel," I said, "I'm
not that kind of a man." She lifted her blouse
a little and pointed to her navel. I don't
remember much after that. Some vegetables were
served. Some pottery was broken. Otto Guttchen
showed me a fossil.

A man stopped me on the street and said,
"Aren't you Victor Hewitt?" "That's me," I
said, "how did you know that?" "I'm a friend
of Julian's," he said. "I don't know any Julian,"
I said. "Julian's Heather's friend," he said.
"Heather Eston?" I asked. "Yeah, I think that's
her name," he said. "So why are you stopping me?"
I asked. "Heather showed me a picture of you," he
said. "Heather has a picture of me? I barely know
Heather Eston," I said. "Yeah, it was a funny
picture, too. You had some fruit on your head
or something," he said. "I never had any fruit
on my head," I said. "That's not something I would
do. I'm a serious guy, I don't put fruit on my
head." "Whatever," he said. "Heather said you
might know somebody who could help me do a job."
"What kind of job?" I said. "Just a job, you know.
A job," he said. "I know somebody who could
help you build a boat. I know somebody who
could help build a house. I know somebody
who could help you build a mandolin," I said. "Very
funny," he said, "but I'm a serious man, too.
And I think you're the wrong Victor Hewitt,

or you're no Victor Hewitt at all." "I find
both thoughts very interesting, Bruno. I really
do," I said. "Hey, how'd you know my name is
Bruno?" he said, "I never told you my name."
"Heather told me," I said. "Wow," he said, looking
like he was trying to entertain a really big
thought, "and I thought I just made her up."
"You did, Bruno," I said, "and so did I. When
two people like us work together, you see how
powerful that can be. I'm definitely interested
in working with you on that job. What are we
going to do, free mice from a lab?" "You're
beautiful!" he said, laughing, while nearly
suffocating me with his fraternal bear hug.

UNEASY ABOUT THE SOUNDS OF SOME
NIGHT-WANDERING ANIMAL

On the way to work this morning, the newsman on the
radio said, "A big part of reality has been removed, it has
been reported. Details are not available at this time. It's
just that, I am told, you will find things different on your
drive to work this morning. Some roads will be missing, whole
areas of the city may be gone. However, the good news is, no
signs of violence have been detected." I turned the radio off.
There wasn't the usual rush hour traffic, for which I was grate-
ful. I wasn't even sure I was on the right road. There were
empty fields where I had remembered rows and rows of apartment
buildings. Then I went into a long tunnel, and I had no memory
of there being a tunnel. When I came out of it, there was nothing,
or, rather, I guess it was a desert, as I had never been in the
desert before. I looked around for signs of the city. A jack-
rabbit scurried across the road, and up ahead a policeman was
leaning against his motorcycle. I slowed down instinctively,
and then pulled over to stop. "Good morning, officer," I said.
"I seem to have taken a wrong turn. Could you tell me where I
am?" "Not exactly," he said. "This seems to be a new area.
It wasn't here before. We're still trying to identify it.
I suggest you drive with caution, because, well, we have no infor-
mation on it as yet." I noticed that he was about to cry. "Well,
thanks," I said. My stomach was sinking. I was certain to be

late to work. I didn't know what to do. Part of me wanted to drive on, to see what was out there, and part of me wanted to turn back, though I wasn't certain of what I would find there. So I drove on for miles and miles, the sand dunes shifting and stirring, and the occasional hawk or buzzard circling overhead. Then the road disappeared, and I was forced to stop, and looked behind me, but that road, too, was gone, blown over by sand in a few seconds. I got out of the car, glad that I had some water with me. I looked around, and it was all the same. Nothing made any sense. I tried to call Harvey at the office on my cell phone. I couldn't believe when he answered. "Harvey, it's Carl. I'm out here in this new place. It's all sand, and there are no roads," I said. "We'll come get you," he said. "But I don't know where I am, I mean, I don't even know if it exists," I said. "Don't be ridiculous, Carl, of course it exists. Just look around and give me something to go by," he said. "There's nothing here. Oh, there was a tunnel some miles back, and a policeman leaning up against his motorcycle. That's the last thing I saw," I said. "Was it the old Larchmont tunnel?" he said. "I don't know, it could have been. I was lost already," I said. "Okay, I'm going to come get you. Just stay put," he said. I waited and waited. And then I just started walking. I know I wasn't supposed to, but I was restless and hoped I might find a way out. I had lost

sight of my car and had no idea where I was. The sun was blinding
me and I couldn't think straight. I barely knew who I was.
And, then, as if by miracle, I heard Harvey's voice call my name.
I looked around and couldn't see him. "Carl, Carl, I'm here,"
he said. And I still couldn't see him. "We've fallen off. We're
in the fallen off zone," he said. "What? What does that mean?"
I said. "We've separated. It may be temporary. It's too soon
to tell," he said. "But where are we. We must be in some relation
to something," I said. "I think we're parallel," he said. "Parallel
to what?" I said. "Parallel to everything that matters," he said.
"Then that's good," I said. I still couldn't see him, and night
was coming on. It was a parallel night, much like the other,
and that was some comfort, cold comfort, as they like to say.

COLLECT CALL FROM NEPAL

I popped myself a beer, and went to sit on the porch
with the newspaper. It was six o'clock in the afternoon
on a Saturday, middle of July, beautiful day. But, then,
the phone was ringing. It was a collect call from Katmandu,
Nepal, from Darcy Symonds. I hadn't seen Darcy in years.
"Yes, I'll take it," I said. "Judson, this is Darcy. Listen,
I'm in a lot of trouble here. There's a revolution going on,
and I need to get out of here. The airports are closed. There's
fighting in the streets. I'm suspected of being a spy and an
informer for the government, but I'm not, Judson, I swear it.
You've got to get me out of here," she said. "Okay, Darcy,
calm down. We'll think of something. How can I get ahold
of you? I need to know where you are," I said. "That's the
trouble, you can't. I'm running for my life. The whole town
is on fire," she said. "Call me again when you know where you
are. Meanwhile, I'll see what I can do," I said. "Judson,
there isn't much time," she said. She hung up. I took a long
pull on my beer and picked up the paper. There was a front-page
story about a two-year-old boy whose dog had saved him from
drowning in the town reservoir. And another about a man who
had found a six-foot boa constrictor in his bed. Police suspected
that its owner will be found. Why would Darcy call me after
all these years? And what was I supposed to do? I tried calling

the State Department in D.C., but they put me on hold and then
switched me over to somebody else, who put me on hold, and so on,
until I finally screamed at an actual human being, "My wife is
trapped in Katmandu. They're going to kill her if you don't help
me get her out of there!" "Calm down, sir. What is your wife's
name?" he said. "Darcy Symonds," I said. "And who is going to
kill her?" he said. "The revolutionaries. They think she's a
spy and an informer," I said. He asked for my phone number and
said he would get back to me as soon as he knew something. I
drained my beer and got another one. I looked at the weather
forecast for tomorrow: another perfect day. I tried to read the
article about the mayoral election, but lost interest. Mr. Giddings
trimmed his hedges until the last light was gone. I ate some
cheese and crackers and a handful of grapes. I waited up most
of the night for Darcy to call back, and also for the man
from the State Department. The phone never rang. I got out my
atlas and looked up Nepal. I read about it in my encyclopedia.
But, still, my imagination failed to picture anything, just
screaming and gunfire and fires, and Darcy's frightened face
I could see, one among the many, running for cover. It was just
another bad movie, and, yet, she was my wife, or so I now believed,
and it had to end happily, safe but for a few scratches, reunited.
I sat there staring at the stars and listening for crickets,

feeling emptier than I had ever known. "Who's in charge here?" I said. "A few good men is all we'll need. We'll need some technical support. You, Jones, take out the Himalayas. Martinez, nullify the Buddha."

THE MIDNIGHT RIDE

Walter Rudnicki was telling me that my little town
was corrupt. "Have you seen the new fire engine?" he said.
"I don't know. I guess not," I said. "That's because there
is no new fire engine," he said. "There isn't?" I said. "No,
the fire department is driving the same old, broken-down engine
it's been driving for the past two decades. The taxpayers
paid for a new one, but you tell me where it is," he said.
"Well, I wouldn't know. I haven't been following this," I said.
"That's the trouble with you taxpayers, you're naïve, you're
too trusting, or, to put it another way, you're fools," he said.
"Now, Walter," I said, "watch who you're calling a fool."
"You know that two-mile section of Stoneham Road that was so
torn up by the ice storms three years ago?" he said. "I don't
get out that way much," I said. "Well, the citizens of this
good town voted to have it paved over. And that's a bundle
of money, let me tell you," he said. "Well, if it needed it,
I suppose that's a good thing," I said. "You don't even know
what I'm talking about, Frank, do you?" he said. "No, Walter,
I don't. I told you I don't have cause to drive out that way,"
I said. "Well, if you did, you'd see that it hasn't been paved.
Now where do you think that money went?" he said. "People can
be lazy, or just forget what they're supposed to do. I doubt
that there's been any malfeasance," I said. "Does the name
Thomas Stolarski mean anything to you?" he said. "I've heard

the name," I said. "You've heard of him, that's great. How
about Noreen Dowling?" he said. "I guess I've seen it somewhere,
on a placard during an election or something. I don't know,"
I said. Walter was pacing around my kitchen, pulling at his
hair. I was sorry I had let him in. Alesia was seated at the
dining room table, finishing her lunch. "Certain people in this town
deserve to be lynched, but I can see that you're not the man
for the job," he said. "You mean, like an old-fashioned, honest-
to-God lynching?" I said. "What other kind is there?" he said.
"My god!" Alesia said. "These people, these elected officials,
stole our money, the money we paid in taxes, and so we're going
to go after them and hang them from trees?" I said, just trying
to make sure I got the facts right. "That's the whole idea,"
Walter said. Alesia joined us in the kitchen. "That sounds
very exciting," she said, smiling. "Are you in or are you out?"
he said. "I love this town," I said. "Does that mean you're in?"
he said. "Can I have some time to think about it?" I said. "We're
going tonight, at midnight," he said, "on horseback." "I don't
have a horse," I said, "but I have a donkey." "A donkey?" he
said. "You can't go lynching people on a donkey." "Then I guess
I can't go," I said. Alesia looked disappointed. I never saw
Walter Rudnicki again. I never even heard anything about the
lynchings. It's a quiet town, and that's what I like about it.
I like the old fire engine, and the beat-up roads.

When I got home from the office, I found that the
elves had rearranged my furniture. At first, I was angry,
but, then, I realized it was a much more sensible arrangement,
and more attractive, too. I wanted to thank the little devils,
but you could never find them when you wanted to. They lived
in the forest right beside my house, and it was dense and
dark in there. Occasionally, I would catch sight of them
running from a neighbor's house, arms full of silver tureens
and pitchers. Usually, they knew I saw them, but they knew,
too, that I never reported them to anyone. So, I guess this
free interior design was their way of paying me back. It's
not the kind of thing you want to mention to anyone else.
"Elves rearranged my furniture, and they did a brilliant job."
"That's great! I wonder if they'd help me?" "I'll talk to them
and see what I can do." That is not a likely exchange. People
are so narrow minded. They walk around with blinders on. We
are small and helpless and riddled with fears. At least I am.
But when I see an elf running with a big silver tureen, I
laugh. I think it's the funniest thing in the world. Once,
in an old junk shop, I bought a dusty old book called *An Elf's
History of the World*. It was twelve hundred pages long. I
took it home and read every page of it. One thing I found
fascinating is that it never once mentions the human race,

not even a world war, of which the elves must certainly have been
aware. As best as I could tell, the book covered tens of
thousands of years, though elves have no sense of time.
They do not mourn death, since they believe in reincarnation—
that is not the word they use, but it is very nearly the same.
The elves stole that book from me years ago, as I believe it
to be very rare; in fact, I have never seen or heard of another copy.
I remember I laughed all the way through it, and wished
more than anything that I could be an elf, mischief and trickery
my main calling. Alas, I was not, and would never be. But
it was a blessing to live so near a band of them. I don't
mind their stealing. Sometimes I buy things I think they'll
like. They love yo-yos and stuffed animals and small shovels.
I respect them too much to ever try and trap one of them,
although my fondest dream is to spend an evening with one,
alone, in my home and for him or her to like me, to look me
in the eyes, and for both of us to speak our hearts, for life
is a serious business, never quite what it seems, and, then,
always more.

THE HORSEMEN

I tilted my head to one side and squinted. I tilted it
back and opened my eyes wide. There was a horseman coming my
way. I still had time to hide, but I wasn't afraid. So I stood
there and waited. He seemed to be riding very fast, a cloud of dust
all around him, and yet he didn't get any bigger. I was growing
impatient. I started walking toward him. I really wanted to meet
this horseman, after all, there are so few left, a dying breed.
I walked faster. Then, I started to run. "Hey," I said, "I want
to talk to you." He was just a dot on the horizon. "Don't go,
I have some questions for you," I said. I looked around. I
couldn't see anything. I stopped running and just stood still.
Maybe he had somewhere else to go. No one said he owed me any-
thing. Of course, it's natural to get your hopes up in a situation
like that. Who wouldn't? I mean, you're standing there in the
middle of nowhere and you see a horseman coming your way, you're
going to expect him to stop and chat with you and you're going
to learn some interesting facts and maybe he'll tell you a poignant
tale involving a woman and child, something you could never have
made up yourself, and at the end of it you're crying and blowing
your nose like an idiot, but you feel good to be so fully alive.
You beg him to take all your money, but he refuses. He thanks
you for listening and rides off with thundering hooves. But that's
not what happened. I got to the edge of town still without spotting

him. There was an emptiness inside me which nothing else could fill. Men and women were tending to their gardens, which suddenly seemed futile and silly. A boy threw a ball for his dog to fetch. He did the same thing over and over. Neither the boy nor the dog ever tired of it. I walked down the street past a high school baseball game and past a church where a wedding party was just spilling out. I stopped and watched the photographer take a thousand pictures. I grew bored and walked on. I wasn't thinking about anything when, suddenly, the horseman appeared out of nowhere and stopped in front of me. The horse was a black stallion with a white blaze on its forehead. The horseman said, "Where were you?" I said, "I gave up." "We waited for you," he said. "I couldn't find you," I said. "I wanted to tell you something, but now I forget what it was," he said. "Your wife and child . . ." I said. "Oh yes, my wife and child were murdered," he said. I looked him up and down. "You don't really expect me to believe that, do you?" I said. "No, of course not. I just thought it was what you wanted," he said. "It was once, but I've moved on. Do you know any funny stories?" I said. "Not a one. I'm the tragic horseman. That's my specialty," he said. "Still, nice horse," I said.

HOUSEFLY

The fly was big and fast and, seemingly, smarter than
me. It would fly right in front of my eyes, and, when
I'd try to chase it, it would land on a crystal vase, or
some other favorite object that I could not possibly swat.
After a while, you feel like an idiot. So, then, I'd decide
to ignore it. I'd pick up my magazine and start to read.
That's when the audacious little monster had the temerity
to actually land on the tip of my nose. It felt like all-out
warfare had been declared. I shooed him away from my nose
and began stalking him in earnest. He dive-bombed me several
times, then flew from room to room to room. Each time he
rested on a window, I thought I had him. But my swats never
even came close. He'd buzz my eyes in triumphant glory, then
disappear without a trace. I was exhausted and angry. That
this lowly piece of insect garbage could outwit me time and
again was inconceivable. The fly has conquered my entire
domain. I am its prisoner. It has proven its point. It
is the superior creature. It spreads disease, malaria and
yellow fever. It sucks blood from sick animals and infects
healthy ones. There are seventy-five thousand varieties of
flies. But this one, no doubt, is the common housefly. I
drag my ball and chain to a chair and collapse. The fly is
gloating atop a bust of Beethoven. What if someone is watching
us? I would be the laughingstock of all time. Even my

friends would abuse me. I would go down in legend. I would become the brunt of a folktale. The fly landed on an oil painting of my mother. It was standing on her eye. There was no end to its cruel taunts. It walked across her lips. She had raised me to be a man, to stand up on my own. I could climb a mountain. I could use a gun. Once I had been forced to wrestle a cougar to save a baby's life. And, now, I was pinned down and humiliated by a fly. The fly was a genius, and a devil to boot. I couldn't give up. I had to fight on. Family honor was at stake. So much had been lost already. I pulled myself up and took a step toward him. He was watching me. He was grinding his teeth and twitching all over. I could feel my strength coming back. He took off and was coming right at me. I swung the swatter as fast as I could and missed him. Then, the chase pursued, from room to room, and several missed swings. A touch of madness had come over me as I knocked over chairs and broke several price-less items. I no longer cared. I had one mission. Now the fly was frightened of me. It realized it had gone too far. Walking on my mother's lips was not funny. It regretted that. He had thought it was all a game. Sure, he had won, but fair's fair. Now, his life was in the balance, with this madman enraged. It's such a short life when you're a common housefly. Nobody likes you. Nobody wants to have fun.

RAKING DAY

It was a crisp autumn day, and I was raking the
leaves in our yard. As fast as I could rake, a strong
wind would blow them all away. But I kept raking, even
though most of the leaves were in the air, in my face and
hair. Kristina was watching me from the living room window,
and I'm sure she must have been laughing. I had been raking
for over an hour, and had nothing to show for it. The leaves
were beautiful in their mad yellow and red dance. Just as I
would think there was some pattern to it, they'd tear off
in a hitherto unprecedented flurry, and for a split second
I'd see a face, and I'd fall in love, or fear for my life,
or both. Then it was just a bunch of leaves in my face that
I was swatting at. Sometimes the leaves would form a tunnel
in the air, and I could walk into it, and wonder where I was
and where I was going, but, then, they'd fly up and away, and
I was exactly where I had been, just more disoriented. I raked
and raked, but not one leaf would stay where I put it. I wouldn't
have another free day for two weeks, and by then it would be
too late. My neighbors would report me to the authorities.
The leaves rise up like a gigantic dragon and spit fire at me.
I rake faster and faster. I'm sweating. I'm weak. I'm
laughing at the sheer aggregate power of the leaves. They
waft me off the ground and blanket me in golden sunlight.

Their hands pass me back and forth from one end of the yard
to the other, and I enter their castles as an honored guest.
And I drink their wine and speak with their god, the wind.
It's getting dark, and I'm dancing with a bonny lass, although
I'm a blind old man and wouldn't know the difference if she
were an ugly witch. It's the dance that matters. Someone
is calling my name from another world. "Lester! Lester
Cunningham! Your dinner is getting cold!"

Jan worked on her book all day, and when it
was time for dinner she said she just wanted a cracker
and a glass of water. I had listened to the sound of
her furious typing all day, and I thought she must be
exhausted. When I finally caught a peek of her, she
looked ravaged. "How's it going?" I asked. "It's not
going well at all," she said. Then, she went back into
her study, and the rapid-fire racket started up again.
I made myself a bowl of soup and read the paper. Three
rabbits had pinned down an old lady on Pine Street and
were just sitting on her when the police arrived. Jan
has been working on this book for six months, and I don't
even know what it's about. I hear her pounding on the
wall and cursing. Once she threw a vase. I feel like
I'm living inside her head, but all I can see is a black
rage and a blacker despair. She types until two or
three in the morning, and when she comes to bed, if I
so much as open an eye, she says, "Don't speak to me,
not one word." My dreams are always about her book, and
they are horrible, gruesome dreams, rampant with torture and
evil. In the morning, I say, "Good morning, sweetheart.
It looks like it's going to be a beautiful day." "You
don't know the first thing about it," she says, and goes off

to work. I drink my coffee and read the paper. Three
men in bunny costumes were arrested for impersonating
rabbits. I start to cry. I cry all day, but very
quietly to not disturb Jan. When she comes out for a
cracker and sees me, she says, "What's bugging you?"
I say, "They arrested three men in bunny suits for
impersonating rabbits." "Those are my characters," she
says. "We'll have to go bail them out." "And what about
the bunnies who sat on the old lady?" I say. "Those,
too. They're all getting away. They don't like me and
they don't like my book." "It's all about bunnies?"
I ask incredulously. "Bad bunnies," she says, "very
bad bunnies."

LETZEBURGESCH

Daphne told me she had heard a rumor that Joel was now working for the enemy. "Who's the enemy?" I said. "Oh, you know, the enemy," she said. "Oh, that enemy," I said. "But Joel's one of us, he would never work for the enemy." "I don't know, I'm just telling you what I've heard. Why would people say such a thing if it wasn't true?" she said. "Joel's a great guy. I've known Joel since I was a kid. And, besides, he has a family, he coaches Little League, he goes to church," I said. "Maybe he needs a little extra money. Maybe the enemy pays better. These things happen," she said. Daphne rushed off for her hair appointment. I wondered if it was her real hair. It seemed tilted, as if it were about to slide off. I placed some stamps in an album, a little packet of them I had received from a stranger in Madagascar. When I finished, I made myself a cup of coffee and sat staring at them, all sorts of lemurs with their long tails and huge, sad eyes. Lemur means ghost. Oh well, who isn't a ghost? I'm not even a real philatelist. I just collect stamps. The next day Joel called to cancel our tennis match. "Is there anything wrong?" I said. "I have to go on a trip, short notice," he said. "Maybe when you get back," I said. "Yeah, sure. Sorry, buddy," he said. There was nothing particularly suspicious about going on a trip, so I thought nothing about it. I hated tennis anyway. But I liked seeing Joel, even if he always beat the hell out of me. He was a natural athlete, so slim and quick and graceful. I stand there frozen, watching the balls whiz by. It's really not much of a game. Some stamps from Luxembourg arrived. I've never met anyone from Luxembourg. It's a country smaller than Rhode Island. Perhaps its citizens aren't allowed to leave. The stamps show fabulous castles and mountains, but pig iron is their real industry. And they speak Letzeburgesch so no one will know what they are saying. I am reluctant to place them next to the lemurs, but I do. Lemurs swinging through the bombed-out castles, everyone has gone mad. I was making myself some tea when Calvin called. He said, "Something big is going down." I said, "Like what?" He said, "I'm not sure, but people are talking, and I've seen some funny movements in the streets. I just thought I should let you know. This could be the big day." "What am I supposed to do?" I said. But he had hung up. I sipped my tea, which always had a calming effect on me. I stared into the eyes of the lemurs. They can heal you if they want to. Perhaps Joel did know something and that's why he left town. I decided to call Daphne. "How was your haircut?" I said. "What haircut?" she said. "I thought you said you were going to get your hair cut yesterday?" I said. "Oh, that haircut. He was closed. There was a sign in the window saying he had moved. I just gave up. It seems like everything is closing. Why is everybody leaving? Where are they going?" she said. "I don't know anything about it,"

I said. "Whenever I go out, everything's still there." "Maybe
it's just me," she said. "They see me coming and they close up."
I pictured her hair sliding off, but quickly put it out of my mind.
"Did Calvin call you?" I said. "Yeah. He takes that job of
neighborhood watchman far too seriously," she said. "He's gone over
the edge. He wants it all to end just so he can say I told you so."
"Daphne, would you like to meet me for a drink tonight at The Goat's
Trough?" I said. "They're closed," she said. Later that night I
went to The Goat's Trough. Joel was there. I went up and sat by
him at the bar. "That was a short trip," I said. "What trip?"
he said. He looked sick. I said, "Are you all right?" "Never
better," he said. "You look a little peaked. Maybe a spider bit
you," I said.

BONA FIDES

Cornell was a great wit and raconteur. He had an effortless
natural grace that made us feel we were all clever. He never
sought to be the center of attention, it's just that we could
never wait to see what he would say next. His wife, Priscilla,
couldn't take her eyes off of him she was so proud. He turned
out book after book, always bristling with intelligence. We all
felt so lucky to know him, to claim him as a part of our inner
circle. Without warning, he died one day. His family, about whom
we knew little, insisted that the funeral be a private affair.
We felt cheated, of course, not being able to say good-bye. He
was buried somewhere far from here. Priscilla wasn't answering
the phone. We all just wandered around in a daze, not really
wanting to get together. Cornell wasn't even cold in his grave—
wherever that was—when rumors started circulating about his affairs,
not just one or two, but perhaps dozens of them, or even hundreds.
His whole life seemed to be an intricate web of lies, and not just
to Priscilla but to all of us. Beneath the surface of charm,
there must have been one scared, panicky animal, always planning
his next deception. I ran into Gwen downtown. "How's Priscilla
taking all of this?" I asked. "She's moved," she said. "She doesn't
want to see any of us ever again. Too painful." It all seemed
so sudden. And then the charges of plagiarism hit the papers.
The articles cited endless instances of pure theft, and his life's

work was discredited, his honor lay in tatters. There seemed to be a kind of awful joy taken in this work. His old friends in town could barely speak of it. "Did you see that article?" "Yeah, yeah." I never took his books down from the shelves to look at them anymore, and eventually I removed them and stored them in a box in the garage. It wasn't long before the rumors and the articles stopped altogether, and then it was as though he had never existed. And, yes, Cornell had more life in him, more good cheer and warmth and brilliance, than anyone I have ever known. I had no way of reconciling what had happened to him, what a swift, harsh vengeance had struck down his memory. I had a picture of him on the mantel, holding his glass up high, toasting the camera. We know now that he was a man of many dark secrets. Maybe his name wasn't even Cornell. Maybe he'd never even gone to school. Maybe he wasn't even a human being. Maybe he was just a piece of tumbleweed that had taken on flesh for a while before blowing on, and he's laughing still. I guess no one ever knew him, but, nonetheless, we all loved him. I was getting all choked up just thinking about him and staring at the photo on the mantel when the phone rang. It was Emory. "Listen, Alex, you're not going to believe this, but I think Cornell is alive." "What?" I said. "I was in the city this weekend and I think I saw him. He's grown a mustache and dyed his hair black, but I'm sure it was him. He was eating lunch

in this little Italian café with this really good-looking babe,"
he said. "I don't believe you, I mean, it must have been some
kind of mistake, just some guy who looked a little like Cornell,"
I said. "It was him all right. I recognized the laugh and the
gleam in his eye," he said. "Did you speak to him?" I said.
"Oh, no, he was no longer the Cornell that we knew. He was someone
else altogether. I watched him a moment, then walked on," he said.
We said good night. It didn't matter to me one way or another if
he was dead or alive. Some of us had been touched by his magic, and,
later, people want to tell you it wasn't magic but a bunch of lies,
you want to ask them, Who are you? Show me your bona fides.
I stared at his photo until it faded from view, and there was
nothing left but dust blowing across the prairie on a cold night
such as this. And then I went to bed.

I said I didn't want any help from anyone, but, then,
when no one offered to help, I was really hurt. Ron called
to ask me if I would help him, and I said no. I felt really
bad about that, but he should have been helping me, and then
maybe I would have helped him. At Sue's house, everything
was broken, including Sue. She couldn't even move. I said,
"I'm leaving now, Sue. I hate to leave you like this, but
I'm late." She stared at me. She was too broken-down to
cry. I could barely walk back to my apartment. When I tried
to turn the key in the door, it broke off. I slid down onto the
floor and started to cry. I felt so defeated. Then my neighbor
returned from walking her dog. "If you could see yourself,"
she said, "you're quite a picture. I hope you haven't been
drinking. I'm no angel of mercy. I hope you don't expect me
to invite you in for a warm bowl of soup accompanied by an up-
lifting speech, because I haven't the time or the inclination."
"My key just broke, that's all. I overreacted. I guess my
nerves were already frayed, and I just broke down. I'll be all
right. I'm sorry to have created a scene and disturbed you in
any way. I have the situation under control now. I just need
to call on the services of a locksmith and I'll be as good as
new," I said. "Well, I certainly hope so. This is not something
my little Muffy needs to see when she gets home from her walk,

is it, Muffy?" she said, and dragged the dog past me and into her own apartment, slamming the door behind her. I pulled myself up and set out to find the locksmith. He wasn't difficult to find. Inside, the old man was busy, grinding something. I stood there patiently, examining the locks he had on display. After about ten minutes, he noticed me waiting. Our eyes met, and then he went on working, making a loud, unpleasant noise. About five minutes later, he stopped and said, "What's your problem?" "My key broke in my lock," I said. "I'll fix it when I get off work," he said, and went on grinding. I continued to stand there. His face was so intensely concentrating on his work he couldn't see me. He was like some crazed cellist, oblivious to the world beyond his own music. I liked watching him create. Sparks were flying as he moved his nose closer and closer to his instrument. His bushy, gray mustache was in danger of catching fire. The grinding sound had given way to a high whirring which he reverberated to a nearly unbearable pitch, and then he took it down slowly until it sung a heavenly lullaby about a faraway forest and some deer and a pond at which they drank in peace as darkness fell. At least that's what I saw as I stood there lost in thought. "What's your problem?" he barked. "What?" I said. "Why are you standing there?" he said. "Oh," I said, "my key broke off in my door. I was wondering if you could help me?" "The shop closes at five. I can fix it then," he said. Then he went back to work. "You'll need my address!" I shouted. He couldn't hear me. So I just stood there and watched him. I didn't know what else to do. It was two-thirty in the afternoon. But I wasn't thinking about time. This old man was working on something that might change the world. He knew secrets that nobody else knew. He was possessed, his eyes ablaze with a terrible private knowledge. I was more and more convinced that he was the only man in the world that could help me. When five o'clock came, he turned off his machine and started to clean up. He finally caught a glimpse of me out of the corner of his eye. "You're still here," he said. "You think your lock is the most important thing in the world, don't you?" "No," I said. "It's a small thing." Then he went and fixed my lock.

SPIDERWEBS

The man sitting next to me on the airplane pulled out
the tray in front of him and set up his laptop computer
as the stewardess gave permission to use electronic devices.
He played the keyboard like a piano virtuoso, but nothing
but annoying clicks came out of it. I read the airline magazine
as if it were a suspense novel, although I glanced at his
screen hoping to decipher something. He was too fast for the
likes of me. Columns of figures appeared, mutated and disappeared.
I was lonely and longed for some good old-fashioned human contact,
but he wasn't having any of that raggedy-assed stuff. I couldn't
even tell what he was trafficking in. When our snack came, he
ignored it. Admittedly, it wasn't much, but still, I devoured it
and stared at his hungrily. He gave me a brief glance of irritation,
stuck it in his pocket, then went back to work. "Fascinating,"
I said. "What?" he said. "I find your work fascinating. Of course,
you've made several mistakes that will come back to haunt you,"
I said. He stared at me as if noticing me for the first time.
"What are you talking about?" he said. "Nothing. It's none of
my business," I said, staring into my magazine. "Who are you?
Are you a spy?" he said. "My name is Jeremy Bendix, and I'm a
human being," I said. "A human being?" he said. "Well, goody
for you. I played golf on Maui yesterday. What does that make
me, a piece of space debris? Now, I have work to do, no doubt
riddled with grave mistakes, but still I'm going to do it, if you'll
excuse me." And, with that, he turned his attention to the screen

and worked more furiously than ever. I nodded off for a while, and when I awoke I looked at him and said, "Oops." He said, "What?" And I repeated, "Oops." He said, "What are you talking about now?" "Nothing, nothing. It's just that you've failed to take into account the effect of the recession in the Southeast Asian market, and the ripple it's had throughout Europe, not to mention elsewhere. Of course, I'm completely out of my league here, and I ought to shut up," I said, and closed my eyes again. "I work hard, but it's not like I'm building a wall of stones that you can see and feel. I'm in the dark, crawling around on my hands and knees. All I can feel are the spiderwebs across my face and the dust beneath my hands. I hear nothing but the chatter of mice and rats. Can't you understand that?" he said. "What?" I said. "Are you talking to me?" "No," he said, and closed up his laptop as we waited for the plane to land. "Listen, I was just kidding when I said that," I said. "Said what?" he said. "About being a human being," I said. "Oh yes, that, of course. I took it in the spirit of jest," he said. I followed him through the terminal and we stood in line for taxis. "Where are you going?" he asked after a while. "I'm going to see a very poor blind man, who rarely eats or drinks, and who talks in riddles, well, not riddles really, but a very special kind of nonsense. He probably knows more than you and me together about the Asian market," I said. "Sounds like my boss on a good day," he said. "It is," I said. "Good, we can share a taxi," he said.

THE SCARAB

For my birthday, Donna gave me a scarab from
Egypt, which she said was thousands of years old, and
said to have special powers. It's a beetle carved from
stone. "What kind of powers?" I asked her. "It'll keep
you from being eaten by the hippopotamus god. It'll stop
you from bumping into pyramids. And it will make you the
sexual prince of the universe," she said. "Those are the
three things I wanted most in life. What a great present.
Thanks, sweetheart," I said. "Of course, that last part
only works with me as your lover," she added. "Believe me,
I fully understood that," I said. "To tell you the truth,
Peter, I have no idea what kind of special powers it's
supposed to have. The man just said 'special powers,' and
I figured anything that old just might have something going
for it," she said. "I like it, and I'll take what I can
get," I said. I put it in my pocket, and carried it with
me from then on. Some days I never gave it a thought, while
on others I carried it in my hand or twiddled with it in my
pocket. I never noticed any surges of power. One day after
my boss had humiliated me in front of several fellow workers,
I grabbed the scarab, and said, "Do harm to him," pointing
it at my boss's back. A few days later, my boss got a call
from his wife informing him that their seven-year-old son
had been hit by a car and was in the hospital. He rushed
from the office in a panic. I grabbed the scarab and said,

"No, no, not the boy. Please make sure he is okay." I was horribly distraught, fearing that I was to blame. After work, I threw the scarab into the river. I told Donna about Mr. Magill's boy, but not about my curse. She could see that I was pretty upset. "He'll probably be okay, just a broken arm or something," she said. The next day, Mr. Magill didn't come to work. But what was stranger, I found the scarab in my pocket. It sent chills through my heart. I went into the men's room and flushed it down the toilet. I asked Wendy Gannett if anybody had heard from Mr. Magill. "Didn't you hear?" she said. "He had a heart attack last night. He's in the hospital, and he'll probably be okay. But isn't it awful?" "Oh my god, this is terrible news," I said. That night, I told Donna about Mr. Magill, and she said, "That poor family." The next day, I was trying to get my work done, because we had all fallen behind, but I was distracted, agitated. I kept looking around the office for something. At first, I didn't know what I was looking for. Then, slowly, it dawned on me. The hippopotamus god was coming for me. I reached in my pocket and clutched the scarab. It was coming, and I was ready.

SPECIAL OPERATIONS

There were some bald men in a field pushing a huge ball,
but the ball wasn't moving. They appeared to be straining
with all their might, but the ball wouldn't move. Then, they
sat down and cried for a few minutes. But, soon, they jumped
up and charged the ball with war cries, and the ball moved a
few inches. They shouted with joy, and jumped up and down,
hugging one another. A woman walked by and stopped beside me.
"What are those men doing down there?" she said. "It's a
warrior thing," I said. "They're working out some technical
problems. They're protecting us from evil, but the plan is
still in the early stages of development." "Does that big ball
represent evil?" she said. "It's either evil or good. They're
still trying to work that one out," I said. "Some men live on
such an exalted plane, it's a wonder anything ever gets done,"
she said. "I meant that as a compliment, of course," she said.
"Only a few are chosen," I added. The men were butting their
heads against the ball and kicking it. "I've always been amazed
that we don't just fall off the planet and float around like so
much space debris. I have a goldfish in my purse swimming around
in a little plastic bag. Would you like to see it?" she said.
I didn't have much choice in the matter. "Sure," I said, "let's
see the little devil." She opened her purse and looked around.
"It's not here," she said, looking terribly distraught. "It

got away, or somebody stole it from me when I was on the bus."
"Maybe one of the bald men conscripted it for the war against
evil," I said. "A fish like that could be used in special
operations." "But it was for my son. He's sick, and I thought
it could comfort him," she said. "Things are different now," I
said. "You'll see, it's all for the better." "I'm feeling a little
weak. I know we've just met, but would it be too much if I asked
you to walk me home. I don't live far from here," she said.
What was I supposed to say? "That would be no problem at all.
By the way, my name is Rudy Byers," I said. "And mine is Paula
Kozen," she said. "How old is your boy?" I said, for the sake of
conversation. "He's nine," she said. A flock of pigeons took
flight from the roof of the hardware store. They flew in a wide
arc, then landed back on the roof in the same spot, all but one,
who landed on the sidewalk to savor a piece of bread someone had
dropped. "What's his name?" I said. "Colin," she said. "What's
wrong with him? You said he was sick," I said. "I don't know,"
she said, "he won't talk. And he won't get out of bed." I was
sorry I had asked. I was trying to take her mind off the goldfish.
"How long has he been like that?" I asked, against my better judg-
ment. "For as long as I can remember," she said. "You could get
another goldfish," I said. "They're cheap." "Do you honestly
think one of those bald men stole it?" she asked. "They couldn't

even move that ball," I said. It was quite a spectacle. "Well, this is where I live. Thank you for your help. I'll be all right now," she said. "Are you sure?" I said. "Oh yes, I have my Colin to look after. I have to be strong for him," she said. "Right," I said. "Well, nice to meet you." I walked back to the center of town and sat on a bench in the park. The flag was snapping on its long pole. Lovers walked by holding hands. A fire engine returned to the station. A dog was waiting for the light to change. Then, it changed.

THE DEEP ZONE

I'm not usually one to nap, but, that afternoon, I was
exhausted, and decided to lie down and give it a try. At first,
I just tossed and turned, thinking of things that needed to be
done. The list was so long it finally put me to sleep. I was
wandering around in a place called the Deep Zone. Moss and snakes
were hanging from the trees, and a sulfurous gas hung over the
ground. I kept walking toward a faint light in the distance.
Unseen birds were clamoring loudly. A man in a green suit tried
to sell me a car made out of possum skulls. I was covered with
leeches, but I didn't mind. A nude woman with long, red hair
walked toward me carrying an orchid. She said, "Vladimir doesn't
like surprises, but, in your case, I'm sure he will be amused."
She smiled as if she knew all about me. Obviously, I was supposed
to follow her toward the light. I looked around for the car
salesman. Maybe that possum skull thing really worked. It didn't
matter, because that's when I fell through a hole in the water
and landed in the back of a Chinese laundry, where I've been
working ever since. When I opened my eyes, it was night. I
didn't know where I was. I thought maybe it was another dream,
and I wanted to be careful not to fall into any traps. They can
be so well disguised you don't realize it's a trap. A pair of
shoes, for instance, can lock shut on you, and you can't move,
and, then, you're an easy victim. An ordinary glass of water,

are you sure it's water, and not some potion that turns you into
a slave? I sat on the edge of the bed in the dark afraid to move.
Something was ringing, a telephone. I stumbled over my shoes,
and turned on the light. I ran into the living room and picked
up the phone. "Where the hell are you, Kimball. You were supposed
to meet me at Packard's at eight o'clock. It's already nine,"
the voice said. "Who is this?" I said. "It's Claudia, who do
you think it is?" she said. "I fell asleep, Claudia. I'm sorry.
I'll be right there," I said, and hung up. I dressed and left
the house as quickly as I could, without throwing caution completely
to the wind. On the way there I thought, how will I know if this
is the real Claudia, or just a simulation of the original? I had
no memory of making a dinner date with her. This Claudia was irritable
at first, but then settled into a more pleasant demeanor. Her
fingernails seemed extraordinarily long, and I had no memory of them
being like that. She kept asking me questions about my work at
Signetco, and I instinctively lied, gave her misleading information.
At some point she said, "Is there something wrong, Kimball?"
I told her I had been ill, and she offered to take care of me.
"I'm better now," I said, "it's just that I'm still weak." When
the food came, she ate like a savage. I couldn't take my eyes
off of her. When she gnawed on the bones, I instinctively withdrew
my arms from the table. "Pardon my manners," she said, "but I'm

starving." Part of me was still back in the Chinese laundry, pressing shirts. We never spoke, we had no common language and this was a comfort of sorts. Of course, there was no escape. Any attempt brought certain death, and not the quick kind either. "You're barely eating," Claudia said. I took a drink of water, and waited for its effect. "You look pale. You're sure you don't want me to look after you for a day or two," she said. "Thanks, but I'm feeling much better," I said. This woman was almost an exact replica of the woman I once knew, and even loved, but something was horribly, horribly wrong. Any fool could see that.

BEHIND THE GREEN DOOR

Thaddeus had said he wanted to get together, but,
then, when we met in town, he didn't seem to have anything
on his mind. "I'd like to get myself one of those remote-
controlled airplanes, and chase pigeons in the park," he
said. "That will show them who's boss," I said. "Of course,
some people might think I'm a little old for that," he said.
"For terrorizing innocent birds? You're never too old for
that, Thad," I said. We sipped at our beers. It was still
before noon, and Mary's was almost empty, except for an elderly
couple at the bar drinking martinis. "They're pretty expensive,"
Thad said. "Martinis?" I said. "No, stupid, remote-controlled
airplanes," he said. "Think of it as an investment in your
lost childhood," I said. He thought that over for a while.
The couple at the bar toasted one another, and laughed. The
bartender brought us another round. It was a Saturday, and
I had many errands and chores on my list. "You know all about
my 'lost childhood,' so I don't need to remind you," he said.
"I can recite what you got and what you didn't get for all
your birthdays," I said. "Then, why do you put up with me?"
he said. "I need to suffer, Thaddeus. It makes me a better
person. So, you see, indulging you is completely selfish
on my part. It doesn't make any sense, but that's how the
world is, and that's why some great good may come out of

making those birds suffer. I don't know what it is, but something tells me it's so," I said. The woman at the bar was tickling the man's ribs, and he was about to fall off his stool. "Then, you think there really is a plan?" Thad said. "Absolutely, right down to the last drop of beer spilled on this floor every night, to the ant you killed walking out your door, and the plane crash in the Andes," I said. Thaddeus seemed stunned, while I was just saying anything that came into my head. I took it as my job to give him something to think about. The couple at the bar ordered another round. Then, Thaddeus said, "If that's true, then I've never really done anything wrong. I had no choice, I'm off the hook." I looked at my watch. We were right on schedule for that conclusion. "And soon the earth will open up, and a ten-thousand-year-old giant squid will strangle us all," I said. "I'm hungry," Thaddeus said, "do you want to get some lunch? There's a new place across the street." "That's not new. They just painted the door a different color. The owner, Herb, had a midlife crisis or something," I said. "Well, then, it's sort of new, I mean, you don't know what you're going to get after something like that," he said. "I see your point. I suppose it could get kind of ugly. Or maybe not. It could be better than ever. Still, I have these errands," I said. "You're afraid to lose even an hour, George, afraid what you might find in its place, something truly unknown, without a name, no visible shape. There's nothing wrong with that, George. You know I've always admired you, so go on your way, get your dishwashing detergent or whatever it is. I'm going to find out what's behind that green door," Thaddeus said. "No doubt there will be an ambrosia burger," I said, "and you'll order one." "I will have no choice," he said. When we stepped outside, the sunlight blinded me. "Good-bye, Thaddeus," I said, "wherever you are." A dog barked, and, then, a siren sped by. I couldn't see my own hand in front of my face.

DEXTER'S LONG SURVEILLANCE

I met Dexter under the old sycamore tree in the middle
of town at three o'clock, just as he had instructed me. He
seemed particularly furtive, looking up and down the street.
"What is it, Dexter? Did you hear something from the police
dispatcher?" I said. "You see that woman over there with the
big hat on walking out of Belinda's Dress Shop. She's the richest
woman in the world, and she wants to buy our town, all the shops
and houses, and all the land," he said. "You called me on a
Saturday to tell me this?" I said. "No, I was just giving you
a little advance warning. Something else is going on which
I was sure you'd find of the utmost interest. See that man
in the sunglasses standing over by Charlie's Pub. See that box
he's got under his arm? Guess what's in that box," he said.
"How am I supposed to know what's in that box? Drugs? Money?
Hell, I don't know," I said. "A head, a human head," Dexter
said. "It's probably just a cake," I said, "a cake for his
kid's birthday." "It's the head of a very famous person, and
he's selling it for a lot of money, believe me, I know what
I'm talking about," he said. "You brought me down here to tell
me that?" I said. "No, I just thought you should know," he said.
People were stopping to talk to the man with the box under his
arm. He gave each one a quick peep into the box. "I still
think it's a cake," I said. "Go ask him for a peek," Dexter

said. "Who's that woman in the black cocktail dress coming out
of the pharmacy?" I said. "Ah, that's Josefina. There are
lots of rumors, but, in fact, nobody knows anything about her.
Many men have died for her, or she's murdered them. It is enough
to see her walk down the street on a day like this. It's rare,
as she is something of a recluse," he said. "I'd gladly die
for her," I said. Dexter smiled. A hearse drove by and honked
at her. She gave the driver a friendly wave. "That's what I
like about this town," Dexter said, "everybody knows everybody."
"I don't," I said. "I mean, I know some, I know a few." "That's
why I like you, Chad. You're a fresh set of eyes. Sometimes
I think I know too much, and it can take the mystery away, and
I'm just a bank of useless knowledge, and there's no fun left
in that," he said. I had never heard Dexter talk like that before,
and I felt sorry for him. "Why don't you just stay home like me
and pursue your private projects?" I said. "See that man over
there in the green blazer crossing the street?" he said. "That's
Percival Bailey. He thinks he's an astronaut. He's walked on
the moon. He has moon rocks in his apartment, and he's happy to
show them to you." "I hope I get to see them someday. But, Dexter,
was there something in particular you wanted to show me because,
if not, I need to get back home," I said. He looked at me.
"There's so much," he said, "look at them. There's an infinite

tango. I can't stop watching, and yet, and yet, I feel so alone."
This was Dexter's way of asking for a dinner invitation. "I made
some beef stew," I said. "Did you know that this sycamore is
six hundred years old? It's the oldest one in the whole country,"
he said. "It's what holds us together," I said. "It's our
secret weapon," he said. "Beef stew," I said. "Beef stew,"
he said.

BLUE SUNDAY

Jaffee was standing outside of Waldo's Café talking
to some raven-haired woman. They appeared to be flirting
with one another. For a man with no visible means of support,
Jaffee lives quite well. He's a regular at the racetrack,
I know, because I'm always there. Sometimes I think I am
following him, and, other times, I think he is following me.
I have no real interest in the man. In fact, I dislike
him. No, that's not true, I'm indifferent to him. It's
just that in a small town like this you bump into people.
And some people you bump into more than others. And Jaffee's
the guy I'm always bumping into. So, you begin to notice
things. Such as this: Jaffee wears the same shirt on the
same day of the week every week. Pink on Monday, yellow
on Tuesday, green on Wednesday, and so on. It makes me crazy.
And, then, I wonder if he's doing it just to make me crazy,
and, then, finally, I make myself crazy just wondering this.
I try to ignore him, but it's impossible. We do our laundry
at the Laundromat every Saturday morning at ten o'clock.
I'll spare you the details of his ridiculous underwear.
He says things like, "Sorry about your garden, Jennings. It
looks like it died a really horrible death, worse than last
year." He knows how much I love my garden. And, besides,
he doesn't even have a garden. He wouldn't have the slightest

idea of what to do with one. So, anyway, Jaffee and this
raven-haired beauty were flirting with one another outside of
Waldo's Café when I walked by carrying a dozen red roses,
which I intended to give to my mother, it being Mother's Day.
I held the roses in front of my face so they couldn't see me.
But, before I knew it, Jaffee grabbed the roses out of my hand,
and handed them to his lady friend. I was so mad I was speech-
less. She threw her arms around him, and gave him a big kiss.
And then they walked off toward her little sportscar convertible.
Every year on Mother's Day this exact scene is repeated.
My poor mother never believes a word of it.

Adam didn't see the flashing lights at the train
crossing, and drove right through it. The train smashed
the tail end of his car, and it spun around rapidly like
a top about ten times before coming to rest. Adam didn't
even know what had happened. The police and ambulance were
there in no time. Over his protests, they insisted he
go to the hospital. He had a few scratches on his forehead,
but that was all they could find. Everyone said how lucky
he was. There was a story about it in the local paper the
next day, with a photograph of his car. When I went to
visit him, he denied any accident. "But there were witnesses,"
I said. "People see what they want to see," he said. "I
wasn't even in town. I was on my way back from the war."
"The war?" I said. "I didn't even know we were at war."
"It's a secret war. Nobody's supposed to know. I shouldn't
be telling even you," he said. I found myself almost believing
him. He looked like somebody who had just come back from a
war, exhausted and drained of any joy he might have once known.
I didn't know what to say. "Were you frightened? Did you kill
anybody?" I said. His eyes had fire in them. "You don't want
to know," he said. "Men, women, children, even dogs, nothing
survived. We had a righteous cause, and we did what we had to."
"What was the righteous cause?" I said. He stood up and began

pacing around the room, rubbing his brow. "I'll never get those cries out of my head, the screaming for mercy, which we were ordered never to heed," he said. I was completely absorbed by his story. He was suffering the guilt of his murderous deeds. "Adam," I said, "some orders don't deserve to be followed, I don't care who gives them." He shot me an alarming glance. "That's easy for you to say, Brian. You weren't there. You were out tending your garden, and mixing your perfect cocktails, while we were being shot at from every direction. I hate to say it, but the commander called me a hero. I saved a lot of lives," he said. "I'm sorry," I said, "I guess I spoke out of line. Listen, I better go. You probably need some rest." "It was hell," he said. On the walk home, I remembered what Adam had said: "People see what they want to see," and I thought, my god, Adam sees himself as a killer and a hero in a secret war, when, in reality, he's just a lucky guy who was nipped by a train. As my mother used to say, go figure, by which I think she meant— oh, forget it. She'd walk out onto the porch and stare at the stars, not sharing her thoughts with anyone, and that's the way I want to be from now on.

THE NEW MULE

One day I was milking my cow, thinking about a pretty
maiden I had passed on the road the day before, when a tank
rolled into my yard and blew my house away. I went right
on milking. A man climbed out of the hatch and jumped down
from the tank. He spotted me in the barn and walked over.
"My name is Lieutenant Lefkowitz," he said. "That's a nice
cow you've got there, a Guernsey, I believe, yellowish milk.
I was raised on it. My mother wouldn't allow Jersey milk in
the house. She got that from her mother, who, in turn, got
it from her mother, and so on. A family has to stand by its
traditions, or where would we all be? Adrift, with no god
to see us through the stormy, dark nights. That Guernsey
milk is powerful medicine. You're living the good life.
Say, would you mind if I stole just a little cup of it. I
have my own tin cup." "Go right ahead," I said. "My god,
that's good!" he said. "Say, I'm kind of lost. I'm supposed
to meet up with my team in the Bash Bish State Forest, but
I seem to have taken a wrong turn." "What about my house?"
I said. "I didn't want you to think I was sneaking up on
you, so I announced my arrival in the only way I knew how.
I saw you in the barn milking your cow. I didn't want to
hurt you, just to say 'howdy,'" he said. "My great-grandfather
built that house over a hundred years ago. My grandmother

and grandfather raised their eight children there, and my
parents raised their five children there. It's all we ever
had, that, and a couple of cows, and some potatoes," I said.
"Well, it's gone now," he said. "I want your tank," I said.
"You can't have my tank. It belongs to the army," he said.
"I don't care," I said, "I want it." "What would you do with
a tank?" he said. "It's miserable in there, dark and musty,
and no place to lie down." "Then, why do you want it? What
are you going to do at Bash Bish State Forest, blow it away?"
I said. "We'll wait for orders. That's all we ever do," he
said. "It's sacred ground," I said. "The spirits there will
kill you, or, at least, make you go insane if you damage one
tree," I said. "I'm a soldier. That's the risk I have to
take," he said. I continued milking Daisy. "It's a beautiful
day," I said. Lieutenant Lefkowitz didn't say anything. He
picked up a hoe and started scratching the ground. Daisy was
eyeing him suspiciously. "My great-grandfather's name was
Jedediah, and he had only three fingers on each hand, but he
built that house by himself. It was my father who put in the
electricity and the plumbing, and I've been living here alone
for the past twenty years since my parents passed away," I
said. "Tradition's all we got," Lefkowitz said. Lieutenant
Lefkowitz was already insane, of that I was fairly certain.

But I didn't know what to do with him. "Memories and yellow milk," I said. "Memories and yellow milk," he repeated. He was walking around, scratching at the ground, in a trance. Tomorrow we would begin to rebuild the house. Daisy would learn to love him. We would grow old together, the three of us. The tank would be our mule. It already resembles one when I squint my eyes.

STRICTLY FORBIDDEN

Clifford told me the headman wanted to see me. "The headman?" I said. "Why would he want to see me? He doesn't think I'm a double agent, does he? Because I'm not. I'm very loyal. I'm not for sale, you know?" "I don't think it's anything like that. I honestly don't know what it's about. It's just that he wants to see you as soon as possible," he said. "I've never even met the headman," I said. "I don't even know if I'll know how to behave. I've always done my best for him. How did he get to be the headman, anyway? Or am I not supposed to ask questions like that?" "You're acting awfully strange," Clifford said. "Ordinarily, I'm supposed to report behavior like yours." "Oh, go ahead, report me," I said. "I don't really care anymore. I do the best I can, but I'm only human. I mean, I'm still human. I walk around, and I have funny thoughts, I can't control them. I try to remember my assignments. I take notes constantly, but then I can't read them. I'm vigilant. I follow people. I eavesdrop on their conversations. But, then, I can't control the urge to be one of them. To just have a normal life, and forget all this other stuff. Is that so bad, Clifford? Is it?" Clifford was writing all this down on his little pad. "Did you say you want to be one of them?" he said. I nodded that I did. "Oh dear, Lucien, the headman does not take lightly such peculiar talk from one of his men. You know I will have to report this."

"I would expect nothing less of you, Clifford. You are a very
loyal man. It's just that, when a beautiful woman smiles at me,
my heart skips a beat, and I want to go home with her. I want
to fall in love and run away, and never have to think about the
headman again. Is that so bad?" I said. "Lucien, you shock me with your
heedless confessions. All these years I thought you were one of
us. I thought you knew the seriousness of our mission, and the
ultimate good that would come of it. Admittedly, it is selfless
work, and requires great sacrifices, but the headman has always
assured us that we would share in a substantial reward someday.
But apparently that is not enough for you now," he said. "And what
will be the nature of that reward, Clifford? Gold bricks in our
caskets?" I said. "It's a matter of considerable importance that
we know what these people are saying and thinking. We are studying
their behavior for their own good. You know that as well as I do,
Lucien. Shifts in habit, new ideas, these are things that can
alter the climate for their own chances of survival. And that's
when we can step in and save them. We play a noble role in the
final balance of power. And that's why we must at all times remain
above them, detached from the domestic brouhaha of their lives.
Perhaps none of this interests you any longer. Am I wrong?" he
said. I didn't answer for a while. Then I said, "No, you're right.
I'm leaving. Perhaps you'll kill me or someone else will. I'll take

my chances. I'm going to try to become one of them, if they'll have me. Maybe I'll fail, and just live in some limbo by myself. But if I don't try, I'll never know. Right now I want more than anything to touch another human being, to be honest and say what I really think," I said. "Well, Lucien, I wish I could say good luck, but I've seen this happen before, I regret to say, and what happened is not a very pretty story," he said. "Good-bye, Clifford," I said, as I walked out the door of his windowless hut. I soon found myself in the midst of a lively crowd of shoppers, and I smiled at anyone who would accept my smile, and several who would not, and I bought a hat from a lady whose hand I touched.

The pressure was on, and I don't perform well under pressure. "You're the champ," Jenny said. "You always succeed. Come on, Travis, you can do it." I stared out the window at the rain. "I'm a loser. I've always been a loser. Even when I've won, it's felt like losing. When I was three years old, I was convinced I would never get anything right. I don't blame anybody. It's just a feeling that permeates my very soul," I said. "But you can do any-thing, Travis. I've seen you. You're amazing," Jenny said. "That's just fooling with people. Sure, I can take a car apart and put it back together again, but what does that prove? I can build a house to keep you out of the rain, but I'm not fooling myself. That's another matter altogether," I said. "You're too hard on yourself," Jenny said. "And what about all those mountains you've climbed? Everyone says you're the best. And all that money you've made through good, honest, hard work?" "That's kid's stuff. Believe me, I'm a loser. I never get anything right," I said.

We'd had this conversation a hundred times before. It annoyed me to no end, not the stuff that Jenny was saying. She meant well, and I knew it. But my part. It sounded so ridiculous. "Why are we even talking about me?" I said. "You started it," she said. "I asked you to kiss me, and you sort of fell apart."

"That's funny, I don't remember that at all. I thought you asked me if I was going to compete in a tennis championship," I said. "I don't know anything about a tennis championship," Jenny said. "I was just feeling a little warm and cuddly, and wanted a kiss." "I'd be more than happy to kiss you," I said. "No, no, the mood's passed. I'm more worried about your soul, why you feel that you will never get anything right," she said. "Did I say that? I've always found that when people start talking about their souls it's best to leave the room," I said. "Do you want me to leave the room?" Jenny said. "No. Of course not. I'm not talking about my soul, am I? Or am I?" I said. "You were earlier, just for a second. I could leave and come back. Or I could leave and not come back. Whichever you prefer. It's your soul. Perhaps you'd like to be alone with it," she said. "I feel like I'm caught in a whirlpool. I'm dizzy and I'm sinking. Isn't there anything we can talk about other than my soul? After all, it's just a butterfly, it's just a poof," I said. Jenny walked into the kitchen and started banging some pots and pans around. I shook my head and stood up. Something was terribly wrong. An egg was hatching in my hand, the egg of an otter. Otters don't lay eggs, but I was starving.

"The lion is back," Lucy said. "I told you, it's
not a lion. It's a bobcat," I said. "Well, whatever,
I saw it this morning sitting up on the hill, staring
down at us," she said. "It won't hurt you. It's afraid
of grown-ups," I said. "Yes, but it carried off the poor
Frasers' little boy last summer," she said. "He may still
be alive somewhere," I said. "And he's killed every outdoor
pet in the neighborhood over the past three years," she said.
"It's much quieter," I said. "Keith," she said, "I think
you're on his side. That's awful." That was the end of
that conversation. I was on vacation. I was supposed to
paint the house, but I spent most of my time watching the
bobcat with my binoculars. I watched him kill three rabbits
one morning, and he popped down mice as if they were bonbons.
I loved his quick, agile movements, never doubting himself,
as most of us do. When I heard Lucy coming, I'd hide the
binoculars, and quickly pick up the paintbrush. "He's there,"
she'd say. "Who?" I'd say. "The lion," she'd say. "It's
his hill," I'd say. I tried not to provoke her, but I often
did. Then, one day she said, "The Meads' little girl is
missing." "Kelly?" I said. "Yes, Kelly. She's not been
seen since Thursday," she said. "What do the police say?"
I asked. "They suspect kidnapping. They're doing everything

they can, but they say they can't do much until there's a
ransom note," Lucy said. "Oh, dear," I said, "this is so
sad." "It's the lion, you know," she said. "Oh, no," I said,
"I've been watching him. He's very content with what he
has up there, rabbits and such." When Lucy went to the grocery
store a little later, I knew I had to climb that hill and
see what I could find. The cat watched me for a while, but
then when I got about halfway up, it disappeared. I wasn't
afraid of the cat, but part of me was afraid of what I might
find. I was out of breath when I reached the top. It was
scraggly and wild up there, full of boulders and fallen trees,
and here and there several caves. I came across the skeleton
of a deer, and then one of a fox, and even one of a porcupine.
I was anxious now, in spite of myself. There was a piece of
blue cloth hanging from a thorny bush. And more bones, bones
everywhere. I knew the cat was watching me from somewhere.
I could feel the coldness of his eyes, and it gave me a slight
chill, as if I had a fever. I called out Kelly's name. And
I remembered the name of the Fraser boy, Adam, and I called
that out, too. Surely they would come and leap into my arms
if they were here, if they were alive. I called again and
again. It was a ghostly place up there, and I had to keep
myself from running. I didn't want the cat to think I was

frightened. When I got back home, Lucy asked me where I had been. "I just went for a walk," I said. "You went up there, didn't you?" she said. "Yes, I did," I said. "It's lovely up there. We should go for a picnic sometime." "No sign of Kelly or the Fraser boy?" she said. "No sign at all," I said. "Just wildflowers and butterflies."

MAP OF THE LOST WORLD

Things were getting to me, things of no
consequence in themselves, but, taken together,
they were undermining my ability to cope. I needed
a hammer to nail something up, but my hammer wasn't
in the toolbox. It wasn't anywhere to be found.
I broke a dish while putting away the dishes, but
where's the broom? Not in the broom closet. How do
you lose a broom? Where was it hiding? And, then,
later, while making the bed, I found the hammer.
Perhaps it was used as a sleeping-aid device. Then
Kelly called and said she had lost her ring last night
and would I please look under the bed. I looked and
found the broom there. So I decided to sweep under
there to see if I could find her ring. I swept out
a rosary, a spark plug, a snakeskin—three feet long—,
a copy of *Robert's Rules of Order*, a swizzle stick,
a jawbreaker, and much more. But no ring. I put the
broom into the broom closet, and started to feel a little
better. I hung the picture and put the hammer into
the toolbox. I made myself a cup of tea, and sat down
in the living room. I had no idea how any of that
stuff could have gotten under my bed. None of it
belonged to me. It was quite a disturbing assortment.

Then I thought of Kelly's ring, and how it could have
fallen behind one of the cushions on the couch. I
drank some tea to calm my nerves. The stuff under
the bed could be the residue of dreams. I drank some
more tea. Then I lifted the first cushion. There
was about three dollars' worth of change and a monkey
carved out of teak. I didn't like the monkey at all,
but I was happy to have the three dollars. Under the
next cushion there was a small glass hand, a lead soldier
in a gas mask, a key ring with three keys, and a map of
Frankfurt, Germany. I sipped my tea. My hands were
shaking. The whole morning was frittering away with
nonsense. I had work to do, or, if not that, then I
should be relaxing. I wasn't going to look under the
third cushion, and I wasn't going to look for Kelly's ring
anymore at all. I sat there without moving, my mind
drifting over the clouds. I was pulling a yak over
a mountaintop, hauling water and rice to a dead wise man,
who knows nothing, says nothing.

It was a beautiful fall day and I was in the park reading a newspaper. A woman with a stroller walked by. She stopped and said, "Do you know what time it is?" "I believe it's about 10:30," I said. "Ever since I had the baby I have no sense of time. I don't even know what day it is," she said. "I suppose you could wear a watch that would tell you all those things," I said. "I never thought of that. Thanks for the tip," she said, and went on her way. I went on reading my paper. A while later she returned. "Excuse me," she said, "but could you tell me where I might buy one of those things," she said. "I don't know what you are talking about. What thing?" I said. "The thing that tells you the time and the day of the week," she said. "Oh, a watch. Well, I suppose right across the street there, at Ellis's," I said. "Thank you so much," she said. I went back to reading my paper. A man with a German shepherd on a leash walked by. "I'm not blind. I just like pretending like it," he said. "I never thought you were blind," I said. "Then I'm a miserable failure. I'm no good at anything. Last week I dressed up like a nun, but I forgot to shave my mustache and people just laughed at me," he said. "Try being yourself," I said. "That's easy for you to say. All you need is your newspaper and people think you are somebody," he said. "I came here to relax. Go on being blind, I don't care," I said. He rolled his eyes upward and let the dog lead him away. I went back to reading my paper. Some sparrows were bathing in the dust around my feet. A while later the lady with the stroller came back. "Look what I bought," she said excitedly. She showed me her wrist. "It's a charm bracelet," I said. "But it tells time, doesn't it?" she said. "Maybe if you held it up to the sun in a certain way you could figure something out," I said. "Oh, good. Life will be so much easier now. You've been a big help to me and I just want to thank you so much," she said. "Not at all. It's been my pleasure," I said. I went back to reading my paper. Starvation. Disease. War. Hurricanes. Tsunamis. I felt like I should be howling and crying and beating the earth. I put the paper down and stared at the sparrows bathing in the dust. The woman with the stroller came back and said, "Excuse me, do you know what time it is?" "It's around 11:30."

"I don't think my watch is working," she said. "Would you take a look at it?" "Well, I can see the Eiffel Tower there, and there's the Empire State Building, and there's a Cadillac convertible. I think it's all there. You should be set for all your needs and dreams," I said. She looked consternated. "But what about time?" she said. "This is a very pretty bracelet, but it doesn't measure time, only dreams," I said. "Oh," she said, looking very dreamy. "Well, I can always ask you, can't I?" she said. "When I'm here I'll always be glad to tell you the time," I said. "Thank you," she said, straightening the baby's cap and walking away. I threw the newspaper into the trash can and walked toward the fountain between two six-year-old hoodlums.

There was a large fat man sitting under the maple tree
in my front yard eating a picnic lunch out of a wicker basket.
He was eating fried chicken, potato salad and plums off of a
red-checkered tablecloth. He looked very content. I watched
him with fascination for some time. I admired his audacity.
But, finally, I couldn't stand it any longer and walked down
to talk to him. "Excuse me, sir, but you're on my property," I
said. "It's lovely here," he said. "Yes, but you're trespassing,"
I said. "I'm going to clean up when I leave. You won't even
know I was here. Would you care for a piece of chicken?" he said.
"I was hoping you would join me, because it's no fun eating alone."
"Well, I was just surprised to see someone out here eating on my
lawn," I said. "I'd read all about you and you seemed like a nice
man," he said. "What do you mean you've read all about me?" I said.
"Well, I work in security and we have all these files. Most people
disgust me, but not you," he said. He was working on his sixth
piece of chicken. "I mean, I don't let those little bad habits
bother me. Everybody has them. Nose pickers, bed wetters, petty
shoplifting, that's nothing compared to what most people do."
"And you read the file on me and decided to picnic on my lawn?"
I said. "That's what I do on my day off, trying to reaffirm the
potential goodness of humanity," he said. I threw down my drum-
stick. "I think you'd better get out of here. I'm beginning to

really dislike you," I said. "The file did say 'Sometimes quick to temper.' I thought you'd recognize in me some kinship. We are partners after all. I mean, you are against all this corruption and greed, aren't you?" he said. He shoveled the potato salad into his mouth with a huge serving spoon. "What I despise most are those files you keep on everyone," I said. "Oh, come on now, they're just sensible. With a society like ours you have every kind of creep and miscreant. We're just trying to protect law-abiding citizens like yourself," he said. "Still, you're trespassing. Thank you for the chicken, but I'd rather you packed up and left," I said. "You're walking the line. You know that, don't you? I know a lot more than I've let on. You're not the squeaky clean man you want us all to believe," he said. "I don't care what you know. I want you to leave this property immediately," I said. He threw his chicken bones around the yard, then folded the tablecloth. He packed his empty bowl of potato salad and tossed the pits of his plums over his shoulder. "This is not the last you'll hear from me. I can assure you that," he said as he struggled to stand. "Pick up those chicken bones," I said. "I certainly will not. You can have those to remember me by," he said. He turned and started waddling up the road. "I'm going to report you," I said. "You don't seem to get it, do you? I'm the big cheese down there. All reports must go through me, you sodomite pagan shithead," he said. And with that he disappeared. I had half a mind to chase him down the street and pummel him senseless. Instead, I picked up the chicken bones and went into the house. He was just a crazy man, I told myself, one of those people who think they're above the fray, when in fact they've already been crushed by it.

THE MASK

My dog, Zeppo, wanted to go for a walk. I opened the
door and there stood a man in a black ski mask. Zeppo jumped
up on him and knocked him off his balance. "Please get him
off of me. I'm terribly afraid of dogs," he said. I grabbed
Zeppo and tried to calm him down. "What do you want?" I said.
"Well, I was hoping to steal something, preferably something
small and valuable," he said. "You mean like gold and diamonds,
emeralds and rubies," I said. "I don't really know. I haven't
thought about it a lot. But I think I'd recognize it if I saw
it. Maybe it's a very rare stamp, one of a kind, worth millions,"
he said. "Well, I don't have anything like that. I have an
old pipe carved from the tusk of a walrus, given to my great-
grandfather by Teddy Roosevelt. I don't think it would be worth
much," I said. "Please don't be offended, but I don't think
that's what I'm looking for," he said. "Well, you might want to
try the Kimballs, a couple of houses down. They've traveled the
whole world, and I think they've collected some pretty fine
treasures," I said. "This is my first time out as a thief. I
feel like I'm off to kind of a bad start. I bought this mask
and I felt real good when I looked in the mirror, but now I
realize that there's a lot more to it," he said. "It takes time,
just like anything. You'll probably spend a few years in prison,
but then you'll pick up some tips and you'll get better at it,"

I said. "Well, how am I supposed to do that?" he said. "I don't know. I'm not a thief. You'll think of something. I have faith in you. You'll probably have to cut some wires or something. Do you have any tools on you," I said. "I didn't think of that. Oh, god, I'm off to an awful start," he said. "I can loan you some wire cutters, but you have to promise to bring them back," I said. "You're too kind to me. How can I ever repay you?" he said. "Well, the Kendalls do have this candlestick. No, I'm just kidding. It's nothing, really. Let me get you those wire cutters," I said. I went inside and found them. "And be careful of the dogs. They have two very mean Dobermans," I said. "And what am I supposed to do about them?" he said. "You'll either have to kill them very quickly or make friends with them by giving them a piece of raw steak," I said. "But I told you, I'm terrified of dogs. I can't go through with this. It's more than I can handle," he said. "And what if the Kendalls are at home? You'll have to kill them, too. Or at least tie them up and gag them," I said. "I would never hurt anybody, not even a dog," he said. He reached up and took off his mask. He was crying. I looked closely at him. It was Mr. Kendall himself. I said, "What did you think you were doing?" He said, "I just wanted to get to know you. We've been neighbors all these years and we've never spoken a word. I was embarrassed and decided if I wore this mask it might be easier. Now I know you for what you are, an accessory to theft and murder." "Why, Mr. Kendall, you are a legend to me. I've always wanted to know you. I've always heard such good things about you," I said. "I'm sorry about the mask. It was a bad idea. It brought out the worst in you," he said. "No, no, I never knew I was capable of such thoughts," I said. "Well, now we've met. We've broken the ice."

It wasn't for everyone. God knows, there was little enough
to go around. I had to fight for my little bit. It got pretty
rough in there. Whoever planned the thing had their head in a
bucket. Before long mayhem broke out. I tried to leave but some-
body kept dragging me back and throwing me on the floor. That's
when I first saw Mary. Of course, I didn't know her name then,
but she was struggling to get up and had a tear in her blouse. I
wanted to help her, but I was in no position. Some three-hundred-
pound lug was sitting on me. I was pounding his chest and screaming.
He didn't care. Hell, he didn't even notice. I saw some guy go
flying through the air, and I realized it was Matthew Quinn, the
organizer. That's when I went unconscious for a few minutes, perhaps
the guy had hit me, I wasn't sure. When I woke, he was no longer
sitting on me, so I tried to stand. I saw this woman, Mary, hiding
under a table, and I started to crawl toward her. Somebody fell
on my back and flattened me. I lay there, trying to breathe. Some-
body bent down and said, "Would you care for a weenie in a blanket?"
"I'd love one, thanks," I said. I choked it down, then tried rolling
the man on my back off me. "Which candidate are you for?" he said.
"I'm still trying to make up my mind," I said. I crawled forward a
little more. A pitcher of lemonade crashed in front of me, splinters
of glass everywhere. So I stood up. Matthew Quinn was standing in
front of me. "I'm so glad you could come. A really good-spirited

discussion is just what we need right now," he said. "Don't you
think it's gone a little too far," I said. "It's important to know
what the other guy is thinking so we can come to a consensus and rally
around the cause," he said. Just then something buckled my knees
and I was on the ground again amid all the broken glass. My hands
and knees were bleeding, but I crawled on toward Mary. Matthew was
knocked backwards and I stopped to see how he was. "My nose is broken.
It's nothing. It's happened many times before," he said. "I think
we're getting close to a consensus," I said. "See, what did I tell
you. It just takes time," he said, bleeding profusely. I was getting
close to Mary. I reached out my hand toward her. She found a steak
knife on the floor and aimed it toward me. "Don't come any closer
or I'll kill you, I swear it," she said. "I wanted to help you,"
I said. "You're an animal, just like the rest of them," she said.
"No, I swear, I had no idea this was going to turn out like this.
I thought it would be a good idea to discuss the issues," I said.
She faked a jab at me and then said, "Yeah, me too, but I don't
think I'm willing to die for them." "My name's Glenn," I said.
"I'm Mary," she said. "Do you think we could find a way out of here?"
I said. "We'd probably be killed or at least maimed," she said.
"Most of the action is in the center of the room right now. Why don't
we crawl close to the walls until we can reach that door," I said.
We crawled over Eric McKenna, who was out cold. Peter Furman smashed

into the wall behind us. I saw Scott Guest fly through the window. And finally we were able to slip out the door. "Those people are crazy," she said. "They're just concerned citizens," I said. That made her laugh. "What were they supposed to be talking about?" she said. "Oh, you know, the usual stuff, faulty mucilage, cross-eyed frogs, obscure birdsongs," I said. "I never heard any of those things mentioned," she said. "They were just warming up to them," I said. "Well, at least they really care about something," she said. "Those are the caringest people you'll ever meet," I said.

THE GANG OF FIVE

Nobody seemed to know what was going on, least of all me.
Billy came over a couple of days ago and said, "I think Martin
is trying to set us up." "Martin wouldn't do that," I said. "He's
one of the most honest, straightforward people I know." "You're
so naïve and gullible, Norman. I'm telling you he's out to get us
all. You shouldn't fall for that Goody Two-shoes pose of his. He's
the most devious man I've ever known," he said. "I stand by what
I said. Martin is a good man. I'd trust him with my life," I said.
Billy left, disgusted with me. I tried to get it off my mind. I
played a game of chess against myself. Of course, somebody's got
to lose. Then I realized that Billy was just trying to get the
suspicion off himself. I didn't trust Billy. Howard called me and
said that he'd seen Nelson walking near the Police Department. I
said, "So what? I walk past there all the time. It's near the deli
that has the best coffee in town, not to mention their sandwiches
and pastries." "He just looked funny, that's all, like he had some-
thing heavy on his mind," he said. "If you want to worry about some-
body, worry about Billy. He's the one that's acting funny if you
ask me," I said, feeling slightly guilty for being involved in such
a conversation. I went to the store and bought a bag of clementines.
I ate three in a row. They were delicious. Rosie called. She said,
"I saw you at the store. You stared right at me and didn't speak.
Is there something wrong? Are you mad at me?" "I swear I didn't

see you. I was so happy they had the clementines that's all I was
thinking about," I said. "Well, it felt like you snubbed me. I
was really hurt and it was hard for me to make this call, but finally
I had to find out what was going on, because Nelson told me that
maybe you wanted out," she said. "Nelson? I never said anything
like that to him. I think some people are just a little stressed
out. You know, maybe we should just take it easy for a while, relax
and smell the flowers," I said. "It sounds to me like you want out,"
she said. I had just spoken up to defend Nelson, and now I hear
he's talking about me behind my back. It really was getting to be
too much. I had another clementine. They were from Louisiana, so
succulent and tasty. Howard called me back. "Rosie tells me you are
thinking about dropping out. It's a little late for that, don't
you think? You have a very important position to play. Without
you the whole plan falls through, and it's certainly too late to
replace you. What are you trying to do to us, Norman?" he said.
"I never said anything about dropping out, Howard. It was Nelson
who put that thought in Rosie's head, and I don't know why he would
say something like that. Maybe he is the bad egg after all. Maybe
he is trying to destroy us," I said. "So now you're blaming it on
Nelson. I swear I don't understand what's going on," he said.
"Howard, you're our leader. It is of prime importance that you regain
your confidence, your steely vision of our plan," I said. "Yes,

yes, I know you're right, Norman, it's just that I'm feeling very fragile right now, like it could all go up in smoke and we all end up dead or in prison for the rest of our lives," he said. "Well, then, let's call the whole thing off. It's causing everyone such nervous distress. To tell you the truth, I was rather content before all this got started," I said. "Yes, it wasn't so bad, was it? This is the first clear thought I've had in months," he said. "And, besides, if we had stolen that statue of Calvin Coolidge, this town would have nothing. It would blow away in the wind," I said.

I cleared my throat and said, "My favorite sport is deep-sea fishing." "That's very interesting," she said. "I had an uncle once who died in a deep-sea fishing accident. It was a very unique case in deep-sea fishing annals. He had fought this sword-fish for over an hour when it leapt from the sea and speared him through the heart. The swordfish was caught, but not by him. He was dead on the spot." "Well, I'm sorry to have brought the subject up. It must cause you great pain to think back on it," I said. "Oh, not at all. He was a terrible bastard. That fish did what we'd all wanted to do for years," she said. "Do you think that fish knew what he was doing? I mean, someone might have even paid him," I said. "The family has often discussed this, but no one will own up to it," she said. "A suicide-fish, trained by the best experts," I said. "Of course, he made sure none of us ever got a damned cent of his money," she said. "I take it there must have been a lot," I said. "He owned three railroads and several sky-scrapers," she said. "And where did the money go to?" I said. "Some whore in Venezuela," she said. "Had you known about her before?" I said. "No one had known anything, but after his death we found out a great deal. Her name was Gabrielle Sabella. He'd met her on a business trip about ten years before. She owned a dress shop in Caracas and, ironically, he had gone in there to buy his wife a present. Gabrielle was from a poor family, but with her extraordinary good looks had moved up in the world. She could no doubt smell Uncle Raymond's money. He never tried to disguise it. What began as a simple affair grew into an obsession. He had to have her and she had to have his money, as it turned out, all of it," she said. "Perhaps it was she who hired the swordfish," I said. "Believe me, we've all thought about this," she said. "Of course, a swordfish doesn't need money. I mean, they don't have a house or a car or kids to put through school. You'd have to have some other way to barter with them," I said. "So Uncle Raymond told his wife, Stella, that he had developed some important business contacts in Venezuela and for the next ten years he flew there once a week for two nights. Gabrielle's demands grew increasingly until, finally, Uncle Raymond put the whole empire in her name in his will," she said. "I wonder how she knew where to find the fish and how did she talk to him?" I said. "What nonsense are you talking about now? Haven't you been listening to me?" she said. "Yes, of course I've been listening to you. How did your aunt Stella feel about all this after she found out?" I said. "She flew to Caracas intending to kill Gabrielle, but the dress shop was gone and Gabrielle Sabella lived in a castle surrounded by armed guards. She waited outside the castle for a month disguised as a poor nun. She had a long knife wrapped up in a basket. Then one day she had a revelation. She realized how glad she was that her husband was dead and she didn't even want his money. It had made him nothing but evil all his days. She took the plane home the next day and has lived happily ever since," she said. "Is she terribly poor?" I said. "Oh, no, she had been salting away her own share of his fortune ever since the beginning," she said. "I hope she had that swordfish mounted," I said. "I'm sorry I ever told you about the swordfish. It was probably crazy anyway," she said.

THE BUG'S REPORT

I filled the saltshaker on the table, careful not to spill
any. Then I screwed the lid back on and replaced the box of salt
in the cupboard. That was strangely gratifying. So I filled
the pepper grinder. One never gets credit for these little deeds.
No one notices. The nutmeg looks a little off today. Perhaps
just having a bad day. A spoon on the counter was begging me
to wash it. I picked it up and then put it down. "I'm not your
slave," I said. Four military jets flew low overhead. I picked
a toothpick up off the floor and looked at it. "You think you're
very clever, don't you, waiting for the perfect moment when you
can exact your revenge," I said. I threw it in the trash. A doe
and her two fawns were eating fallen apples in the backyard. Some-
times I see them when they're not there. I walk into the living
room and rearrange the pillows on the couch—red, black, yellow.
I can only stand to have them that way, but other people have
other ideas, bad ideas. I sat down in my chair and closed my
eyes. For one minute I dreamed I was a pauper on the streets
of Paris happy with my crumb of bread. I opened my eyes and saw
a ladybug tracing crazy eights in front of me. I watched with
fascination until it landed on my hand and began to explore
each finger. It was a creature of endless curiosity. When it
finished with my hand it flew away back to headquarters to file
its report: Large Hairy Hand, Clean Nails, Belonging to an

Immobile Giant of No Great Account. But I want to be loved and admired, even by bugs. What a desperate creature man is, or, no, not man, I am. I walked to the window and watched old Mrs. Delaney hang her laundry. She's not even five feet tall and has to stretch to reach the line. Her white hair is permed and she's wearing an old housedress, the print so faded it hardly exists. I went back into the kitchen and washed the spoon. "Are you happy now?" I said. I looked out the window. The doe and two fawns were gone, but their ghosts remained.

When the little man opened his mouth he squawked like a bird. So I grabbed him by the shoulders, spun him around and threw him down the steps. I ran down the steps and picked him up. He had a bump on his forehead, but, other than that, he seemed to be in fine shape. "What do you say now?" I said. "Was it that bit about the Queen that ticked you off?" he said. I socked him in the eye. Then I socked him in the other eye. He squawked and fell to the ground. I picked up his feet and dragged him across the floor. "Stand up," I said. His legs thrashed around a bit, but finally he was able to stand, swaying slightly. "Do you suppose I could have a glass of water?" he said. "Certainly," I said, and fetched him his glass of water. I watched him gulp it down, and then I said, "See this hammer. I am going to hit you on the head with it." "That will surely hurt," he said. I raised the hammer and brought it down on his head. Again, he slumped to the ground. I made myself a cheese sandwich and ate it in the other room. When I went back he was still out, so I filled up his water glass and threw it in his face. He opened his eyes and looked at me. "Who are you?" he said. "Never mind who I am. Stand up. You spend far too much time napping. It's not good for you," I said. He struggled and fell over several times. Finally, I lent him a hand and he made it to his feet. I picked the whip off the chair. "You're going to like this," I said. "Turn around." I lashed him a good one. He let out a squeak. I lashed him twenty times all told. Blood soaked through his shirt. "Oh my," he said, "you are certainly an expert with that device." "Why, thank you," I said, "I do take a certain pride in my technique." He was covered in sweat and his hair was standing on end. "Perhaps you would like a little rest before we move on to the next step?" I said. "A little rest would be most welcome," he said. "Have a seat," I said. He was breathing rather heavily. Both his eyes were black. "It has occurred to me, sir," he said. "Of course, the matter of an explanation is strictly voluntary." "I don't owe it to you," I said. "Oh, yes, sir, I understand that," he said. "However, since you have been so cooperative, I will tell you this: it has nothing to do with the Queen," I said. He stared at me with his mouth open. "That's it, that's all you're going to tell me?" he said. "Don't you feel better now?" I said. "Yes, sir. Thank you, sir," he said. "Well, I think we've had enough of a rest. Back to work," I said. I threw him against the wall, then kneed him in the stomach. I threw him back against the wall, then smashed him in the face. When he fell to the floor, I kicked him in the ribs. He laid there moaning and sputtering. I lay down beside him. "You're quite a remarkable man, you know," I said, "with many admirable qualities. The Queen would like to meet you for tea. She's a single lady now that her husband, the King, has died. She's very attractive for her age, which I believe is the same as yours. I don't mean to put any ideas in your head, but I hope you'll think it over," I said. "Over my dead body," he said.

THE ENEMY

I have searched for a way out, but without success. I saw
in the clouded mirror the tatters of a once bright future. I felt
as though I had squandered something precious and rare. What I
had known of friendship was mine no more. Even the poorhouse
wouldn't take me. I tried to huddle with the homeless and they
beat me with sticks. So I joined the army and that's when my luck
started to turn around. I was promoted right away. I was an ideal
soldier. I followed orders. I said, "Yes, sir. No, sir." There
was nothing I wouldn't do to please my officers. I dug ditches.
I climbed ropes. I could shoot the bull's-eye out of targets all
day long. Then one day we went to war. I was beside myself with
anticipation. The enemy loomed large in my head. I was going to
get a whole chest full of medals. The first day out on patrol
we didn't see anybody. Oh, some kids threw rocks at us, and an
old man on a donkey pretended not to see us. A couple of shots
were fired, but who knows at what. That night, in camp, a bomb
exploded, killing three. The second day out I narrowly missed
stepping on a mine. My heart was racing. Suddenly I was afraid.
We searched building after building without results. I said to
a fellow soldier from Kansas, "Where the hell are they?" He said,
"They're everywhere. They're all around us, watching, seeing
our every move." "Well, why don't they do something?" I said.
"They don't need to. We're doing exactly what they want us to,"
he said. We walked on, kicking the sand. The heat was unbearable
and I was starting to see things. But I knew better than to fire

my weapon. A rocket went whizzing overhead and exploded, just
missing us. "It came from over there," I said to Kansas. "Don't
worry, you'll never find him. He's gone," he said. A woman was
filling her jug at a well. We fanned out and circled an old church.
"They like to hide in churches," I said to Kansas. "Don't count
on it," he said. I flung open the door, my rifle at the ready.
Several old people were on their knees praying. They turned and
looked at me. "Sorry," I said. The captain received a report
that there were enemy forces hiding among the rubble not far from where
we were. We approached cautiously. A shot was fired and we opened
up, rifles blazing enough to deafen you. We kept it up for several
minutes. Then all fell silent and a scout was sent to check it out.
There was nothing there, except some old tin cans and a hubcap.
That night we sat around a campfire and sang. It felt good to
be in the company of real men. I was proud to belong. In the
morning five soldiers were found dead in their tents, their throats
slit. I was so mad I could taste blood. Revenge was our mission.
We strode through town, kicking open doors, scaring people out of
their minds, looking through every room. After hours of this, we
found nothing. I said to Kansas, "What are we doing wrong?" He
said, "You still don't get it, do you? We're the enemy." I was
confused. We regrouped and left the village. One soldier was
startled by a shadow and fired at it.

CLEANING OUT THE DESK

I was working at my desk, straightening papers and throwing
things away. I opened one drawer and there was a paper bag with
a baloney sandwich in it that must have been three years old. I found
some notecards with hieroglyphics carefully written on them. I
also found an envelope containing a clip of someone's hair. It
must have been the hair of someone I loved once, but I couldn't
remember. Then there was a long letter from someone named Seth,
accusing me of stealing his material and making a fortune off of
it and never giving him a dime. First off, I have never made a
fortune from anything, and secondly, I'm not a thief. I don't even
know what kind of material he is referring to. The letter's dated
ten years ago. I tossed it in the trash. I kept digging. There
were photographs of children, distant relatives of mine, but I'd
never met them and didn't know their names. Perhaps they'd visit
me in my old age, not that I wanted them to. And here is a postcard
from Lola. The next day she rode a horse off into the mountains
and was never heard of again. My darling Lola, she had such plans.
There was a small jade Buddha in the back of the drawer. I remember
I carried it for luck for many years. I don't know why it ended
up back there, retired or punished. In another drawer I found
notes on the Oracle of Delphi, "Man, know thyself and be divine,"
and a map of the Delaware River. I seem to remember a plan to go
exploring there. Then a stack of letters from my old friend Beverly
Babcock. She moved to Greece and fell in love with a fisherman.

The letters stopped and mine were returned. She had trained to
be an opera singer and I thought her voice was quite good. I guess
I loved Beverly, but I never told her. Beneath her letters there
was a guide to the subway systems of Antwerp. That would come in
handy if I ever went to Antwerp. There were several old coins
in plastic bags. And a postcard from Denise in Hawaii saying they
were having a great time, and wishing I was there. There was an
antique toy milk truck with half its paint chipped off. I
remembered it from my childhood. Why would I save a thing like
that? It troubled me to think about it. I shut the drawer and
broke for lunch. I made myself a sandwich and sat down at the
table. It's funny, I never believed Lola died in the mountains
of Arizona. I thought she got herself another identity. I imagined
that she had something dark in her past that she was trying to
escape. That was just my way of keeping her alive a little longer.
And Beverly, I can see her singing in church in that small fishing
village on holidays, her man looking on proudly. I wonder if she
ever thinks of me. I got up and washed my plate. That little
milkman was a terrible driver, always crashing into walls and
falling off of tables. We were poor and it was all I had to amuse
myself. Poor milkman, such a lousy driver, but he's followed me all
these years. The President is missing, I thought. "Oh no," said
the Secretary of State, "the President has a very busy schedule
and he has been temporarily misplaced. We will find him, I assure
you." "But he's missing," I said.

MY BRUSH WITH GREATNESS

I met Phongsri Kwanmuang. He seemed like a very calm, wise
man. He also knew how to make a nuclear bomb. I invited him
over to my house for tea. He said, "Do you want to make a bomb
together?" I said, "Oh, no, I have no use for a bomb. Perhaps
we could do something else, like go bicycling." "I do not know
how to bicycle. I am afraid of the bicycle. It looks like it
could eat me," he said. "Well, there are plenty of other things
we could do, like hiking or bowling," I said. "I tried bowling
once. It nearly killed me. I think making bombs is the only
thing I like to do," he said. We finished our tea. Phongsri
thanked me. "You are most kind to have me in your house. It is
my hope that we can be friends," he said. He bowed and departed.
I didn't think about him after that. About a month later he showed
up at my door. He said, "You don't like me. You never called or
came by to see me." I said, "Oh, I've been busy. You know,
it's the end of the semester, all those papers to grade." "You
think I'm a bad man because I make bombs. That's it, isn't it?"
he said. "No, Phongsri, you're wrong. Bombs are your business.
That's what you do. What business is it of mine?" I said. "I'm a
lonely man. I miss my family, my wife and children. The university
pays me so much more than I can make at home, but nobody speaks
to me. It is as if I am radioactive. Who knows, perhaps I am
by now," he said. "Would you care for some tea?" I said. Phongsri
eagerly accepted. It became clear to me that he barely knew where
he was. He didn't know who was president, had never heard of the

World Series or the Rolling Stones. He lived in a very tiny world, but he knew how to blow it up. "Phongsri," I said, "I think you need to get out more." "What do you mean by 'get out'?" he said. So I started taking him out every Saturday night. We went to the theater. I took him to concerts. We went out to dinner. I even took him to several bars. He was reluctant to drink at first, but once he gave in he seemed to enjoy it. One night he said, "You know, Tom, I've never felt so alive. I have to thank you. You have given me a gift." "It has been wonderful to watch you open up, Phongsri," I said. He was staring at our waitress, who was wearing a provocative black swimsuit. "I must have her. I am deeply in love with her," he said. "Phongsri, she's just a waitress. Leave her alone," I said. "No, you must not tell me what to do. This is my destiny," he said. "Let's go, Phongsri. You've had too much to drink," I said. I grabbed him by the arm and dragged him out of the place. He was struggling against me all the way. After that night, I never saw him again. At the end of the year he won the Nobel Peace Prize, which I never could figure out. But that was my brush with greatness. It left me kind of hollow inside. I dated that waitress for a while, but she left me for a drummer.

I said, "I want to go home." "I told you, we have no home,"
Anne said. "What happened to our home?" I said. "The government
took it," she said. "What for?" I said. "They said it was for
strategic reasons," she said. And, thus, we commenced our roaming.
Mostly we stayed at campsites along the way. We had a tent and
sleeping bags, a couple of pots and pans. I was confused about what
had happened to us, but I also liked the adventure. Once a man
came over and said that he and his wife would like to share their
dinner with us. Anne said her husband wasn't feeling well. I said,
"I feel great." We sat around their campfire and talked. The man
said he used to be a dentist, but now he was a gold miner. "You
should've been taking those little gold caps out of people's
mouths all along. You'd be rich now," I said. Anne plowed
her elbow into my ribs. "We're headed for the Klondike," his
wife said. "It's best to stay out of the strategic zones," Anne
said. They nodded in unison. "But I still don't know where they
are," I said. They all looked at me, but didn't say anything.
We ate some awful, strange meat and some baked beans, at least I
think that's what they were. Later that night I was sick. In the
morning when we had been on the road about three hours a band of
Indians came riding toward us. "What are we supposed to do?" I
said to Anne. "They've risen up all over the country. They're
on the warpath. They're going to take over the government," she

said. "But what about us right now?" I said. "Just be nice,"
she said. When they came along side of the car, Anne stopped
and rolled down her window. "Howdy, fellow Americans," she said.
"Can you tell us how to get to Topeka?" he said. "Sure, that's
easy," she said, and proceeded to give him directions. "That's
most helpful," he said. "Have a good day." We drove on into
the glaring sun. "Where are we going?" I said. "Do I look like
I know where we're going? I just want to get away as far as we
can," she said. "What about our old friends?" I said. "You'll
just have to make new ones," she said. "Patagonia, is that where
we're going?" I said. "No, we're not going to Patagonia. I don't
know where we're going," she said. "We're getting low on gas and
I don't think there's going to be a station for a long time," I
said. "Then we'll have to walk," she said. I was beginning to
see how crazed she was and it frightened me. "We don't have
anything to eat," I said. "You can kill a jackrabbit," she said.
There was an old shepherd up ahead moving his flock across the
road. When we pulled to a stop, she said, "Get out and grab one
of those sheep and throw it in the backseat." I said, "I'm not
going to do that. There's no way." She looked at me, then opened
her door, and went and grabbed a sheep around its waist and tried
to heft it up. She dropped it and tried again. It took all her
strength to drag it over to the car. She finally managed to

stuff it in the backseat before the shepherd saw what she had done. He pounded on her window and hit it with his staff. "A curse on you. I put a curse on you!" he shouted. She rolled down her window and yelled back at him, "National Security. It's for your own good."

I didn't understand what was expected of me. Maxwell told
me to walk around with an orchid in my hand and then I would be
counted. I did this and then this woman came out and said, "Where's
your teddy bear?" "I was told to bring an orchid," I said. "Orchids
come much later. Right now it is only a teddy bear that counts,"
she said. I started to leave, feeling slightly annoyed. Maxwell
spotted me and came running up. "What are you doing with an orchid?"
he said. "You told me," I said. "Not now, for god's sake. This is
the teddy bear stroll," he said. "I know, I know. I don't know
if I'm up to this thing," I said. "You don't have any choice. It's
required," he said. When I came back clutching my teddy bear,
people were standing around in pairs taking turns slapping one
another. There were no teddy bears in sight. The couples didn't
speak. There were significant pauses between slaps. A man walked
up to me and said, "Where's your partner? Why aren't you slapping?"
I said, "I don't have a partner." "Of course you have a partner.
Everybody has a partner," he said. "I was out getting my teddy
bear," I said. "Teddy bears have got nothing to do with it. This
is the slapping time," he said. I looked around everywhere. There
was one small little girl crawling around in the grass, but I didn't
want to slap her. I drifted away and walked around the block. When
I came back they were sitting on the ground in a straight line. The
first one would start to howl, then the second one, and so on down

the line, each taking their turn. I went and started to sit at
the end of the line, but the man said, "No, no, I'm the last. So
you can't sit here. This is my place." I looked down the line and
realized that everybody was attached to their exact position. I
looked around for Maxwell. I was so confused. Why was I required
to be here when I didn't fit into anything. I saw the little girl
still crawling in the grass. I went over and sat down beside her.
"What are you?" I said. "I'm a snake and I'm going to bite you,"
she said. "Bite me and get it over with," I said. So she crawled
up to me and bit me on the leg. It hurt. "You're going to die
now," she said. "I figured as much," I said. The howling had
stopped. I turned around. They were taking turns diving through
hoops of fire. I decided I didn't want to belong to the human race
so I started making snake-like movements in the grass. Suddenly
Maxwell was standing there. "You've failed this whole thing. I
tried to tell you what to expect and look at you," he said. "I'm
a snake," I said. "You're a very poor snake," he said.

THE UNDERGROUND

There was a little boy sledding down the hill out there.
Even though I couldn't hear it, he was yelling and screaming.
He was going pretty fast and steering pretty good, missing certain
obstacles. I thought sure he'd turn the sled over, but he didn't.
He made it all the way to the bottom, then he stood and started
trudging back up the hill again. I watched him repeat this operation
five times before darkness started to fall and his mother called
him in. His mother's name was Gloria Grover, and she had once
been a part of the underground. I don't know what she did, but
I'd see her at meetings, and sometimes she would disappear for
a month or two. She looked very different back then, dressed
all in black with a leather coat. Now she looked so matronly,
not unattractive, but like a good mother. I know I look very
different, too. Not that the underground has broken up, it's just
passed on to the younger generation. I sometimes see the work they've
done, and it's good. But most of the time it's the invisible stuff
that matters, like breeding new insects to infiltrate the brains
of our rulers. I really got a kick out of that one when I heard
about it. One of the big shots would appear on TV and he'd be
telling us what a great job he was doing for us and suddenly his
eyes would go blank and he'd say, "Carumba diddle do, I have lied
to you. I just want to be a cowboy." And then he'd start crying
and they'd take the camera off of him and insert a cartoon. Eric
Sanborn came by the other day and told me he caught his postman
tiptoeing through his house reading letters and looking in his

address book. "What did you do to him?" I asked. "I tied him up and gagged him and threw him in the basement," he said. "That's a bit harsh. He was just doing his job," I said. "Well, I'm just doing mine," he said. "But I thought we had given that up," I said. "There's just so much you can take," he said. "Don't worry, I'm not going to hurt him, though there could be a few rats down there." I don't know if Gloria Grover remembered me. She saw me drive by her house regularly and occasionally she'd smile and give me a wave. But that's what neighbors do. I never saw her husband if she had one. The next day I saw her son climb the hill with his sled bright and early. That's what he lived for now, the speed and thrill of descent. It was the first year he'd been able to do it alone. I loved standing by the window watching him. One day the President said that the elections would be canceled. He said it was just too dangerous at this time. I turned off the radio and looked at the falling snow. I couldn't get out if I wanted to. Gloria stood at her door calling her child, Mickey, I think was his name. He didn't come. I looked over the hill. I didn't see him at first. And then I saw that he had crashed into a snow-bank. I grabbed my coat and ran out the door. I got there just as she did. She pulled him out and picked him up. He opened his eyes and smiled at her. "That was spectacular. Did you see it?" he said. "Yes, honey, you scared me to death," she said. Then she looked at me and said, "You're him, aren't you?" "Yes," I said. "Well, it's time we did something," she said.

TO ADVANCE NO FARTHER INTO THE
RUBBLE OF THE BUILDING

When I was in the grocery store a man came up to me and said,
"My, I admire your hat. Do you mind if I ask you where you got it?"
"I was in the Polish Army. I got it there," I said. "Well, I was
in the Polish Army, too. May I ask what regiment you were in?"
he said. "I was in the 172nd Regiment, infantry," I said. "That's
exactly what I was in. I never saw any hat like that," he said.
"Well, I'm sorry for you. Maybe you were sick or sleeping or away
on leave the day they handed out these hats. But, you're right,
it is a fine hat, keeps you warm in all kinds of weather," I said.
"I want that hat," he said, reaching for it. I grabbed his arm and
twisted it. "You're hurting me," he said. "Don't ever reach for
this hat again or I'll break your arm next time," I said. He looked
frightened and backed away from me. I threw some potatoes into
my basket and moved on. A little while later a woman came up to
me and said, "I just want to touch your hat. You saved my village.
I think I even remember your face. You were so brave in the face
of such a fierce enemy. You should let me buy you a bottle of the
best champagne." "I don't think we saved anything. We were really
outnumbered and outgunned," I said. "No, that's not true. You
were so brave and courageous," she said. "That was a long time
ago. I have forgotten many of the details," I said, and tried to
push past her. I was at the meat counter, studying the pork chops.
"I'll have those two fat ones," I told the man. "Are you Brownie

Kaczenski?" he said. "No, but I knew Brownie many years ago. He was killed in the war," I said. "Oh, that's too bad. I grew up with Brownie, and I lost track of him after he joined the army. You look just like him, or what I thought he would have looked like if he had survived. I'm sorry to hear about Brownie, but glad you made it out alive. My family just barely got out," he said. He handed me my pork chops. I picked out some bread and cheese and was about to head for the checkout counter when a man pushed his cart in front of mine and said, "I ought to break your neck right here in front of everybody, you low-down, vicious killer. You killed my brother. I'd never forget your face." "I never killed anybody. I was on the run for most of the war. You've got the wrong man," I said. "You're a liar. I remember your face. I was just a little kid crouching behind the barn, but I know what I saw and it was you," he said. "You're mistaken, mister. I had a brother who was in the war and we looked a lot alike, but he was killed, too, just like your brother. I'm sorry, but it wasn't me I can assure you," I said. "Okay, killer, go on, but don't let me ever catch you in a dark alley," he said. I went up to the checkout counter and paid for my groceries. The clerk kept staring at me. "Is there something wrong?" I said. "It's the hat," he said. "Did you get it around here?" "No, I was in the Polish Army," I said. "Oh, cool," he said.

I answered the ad in the paper. I had been unemployed for
nine months and was desperate. At the interview, the man said,
"Do you have much experience climbing tall mountains?" "Absolutely.
I climb them all the time. If I see a tall mountain, I have to
climb it immediately," I said. "What about swimming long distances
in rough ocean waters, perhaps in a storm?" he said. "I'm like
a fish, you can't stop me. I just keep going in all kinds of
weather," I said. "Could you fly a glider at night and land in
a wheat field, possibly under enemy fire?" he said. "Nothing
could come more naturally to me," I said. "How are you with
explosives? Would a large building, say, twenty stories high
present you with much difficulty?" he said. "Certainly not. I
pride myself on a certain expertise," I said. "And I take it you
are fully acquainted with the latest in rocket launchers and land-
mines?" he said. "I even own a few myself for personal use. They're
definitely no problem for me," I said. "Now, Mr. Strafford, or may
I call you Stephen, what you'll be doing is driving one of our ice
cream trucks, selling ice cream to all the little kids in the
neighborhood, but sometimes things get tricky and we like all our
drivers to be well-trained and well-equipped to face any eventu-
ality, you know, some fathers can get quite irate if you are out
of their kid's favorite flavor or if the kid drops the cone," he
said. "I understand, I won't hesitate to take appropriate action,"

I said. "And there are certain neighborhoods where you're under advisement to expect the worst, sneak attacks, gang tactics, bodies dropping from trees or rising out of manholes, blockades, machine gun fire, launched explosives, flamethrowers and that kind of thing. You can still do a little business there if you are on your toes. Do you see what I'm saying?" he said. "No problem. I know those kinds of neighborhoods, but, as you say, kids still want their ice cream and I won't let them down," I said. "Good, Stephen, I think you're going to like this job. It's exciting and challenging. We've, of course, lost a few drivers over the years, but mostly it was because they weren't paying attention. It's what I call the Santa Claus complex. They thought they were there just to make the kids happy. But there's a lot more to it than that. One of our best drivers had to level half the city once. Of course, that was an extreme case, but he did what needed to be done. We'll count on you to be able to make that kind of decision. You'll have to have all your weapons loaded and ready to go in a moment's notice. You'll have your escape plans with you at all times," he said. "Yes, sir, I'll be ready at all times," I said. "And, as you know, some of the ice cream is lethal, so that will require a quick judgment call on your part as well. Mistakes will inevitably be made, but try to keep them at a minimum, otherwise the front office becomes flooded with paperwork," he said. "I can assure you I will use it only when I deem it absolutely necessary," I said. "Well, Stephen, I look forward to your joining our team. They're mostly crack professionals, ex–Green Berets and Navy Seals and that kind of thing. At the end of the day you've made all those kids happy, but you've also thinned out the bad seeds and made our city a safer place to be," he said. He sat there smiling with immense pride. "How will I know which flavor is lethal?" I said. "Experiment," he said. I looked stunned, then we both started laughing.

Someone had spread an elaborate rumor about me, that I was
in possession of an extraterrestrial being, and I thought I knew who
it was. It was Roger Lawson. Roger was a practical joker of the
worst sort, and up till now I had not been one of his victims, so
I kind of knew my time had come. People parked in front of my
house for hours and took pictures. I had to draw all my blinds
and only went out when I had to. Then there was a barrage of
questions. "What does he look like?" "What do you feed him?" "How
did you capture him?" And I simply denied the presence of an
extraterrestrial in my house. And, of course, this excited them
all the more. The press showed up and started creeping around
my yard. It got to be very irritating. More and more came and
parked up and down the street. Roger was really working overtime
on this one. I had to do something. Finally, I made an announcement.
I said, "The little fellow died peacefully in his sleep at 11:02
last night." "Let us see the body," they clamored. "He went up
in smoke instantly," I said. "I don't believe you," one of them
said. "There is no body in the house or I would have buried it
myself," I said. About half of them got in their cars and drove
off. The rest of them kept their vigil, but more solemnly now.
I went out and bought some groceries. When I came back about an
hour later another half of them had gone. When I went into the kitchen
I nearly dropped the groceries. There was a nearly transparent

fellow with large pink eyes standing about three feet tall. "Why did you tell them I was dead? That was a lie," he said. "You speak English," I said. "I listen to the radio. It wasn't very hard to learn. Also we have television. We get all your channels. I like cowboys, especially John Ford movies. They're the best," he said. "What am I going to do with you?" I said. "Take me to meet a real cowboy. That would make me happy," he said. "I don't know any real cowboys, but maybe we could find one. But people will go crazy if they see you. We'd have press following us everywhere. It would be the story of the century," I said. "I can be invisible. It's not hard for me to do," he said. "I'll think about it. Wyoming or Montana would be our best bet, but they're a long way from here," I said. "Please, I won't cause you any trouble," he said. "It would take some planning," I said. I put the groceries down and started putting them away. I tried not to think of the cosmic meaning of all this. Instead, I treated him like a smart little kid. "Do you have any sarsaparilla?" he said. "No, but I have some orange juice. It's good for you," I said. He drank it and made a face. "I'm going to get the maps out," I said. "We'll see how we could get there." When I came back he was dancing on the kitchen table, a sort of ballet, but very sad. "I have the maps," I said. "We won't need them. I just received word. I'm going to die tonight. It's really a joyous occasion, and I hope you'll help me celebrate by watching *The Magnificent Seven*," he said. I stood there with the maps in my hand. I felt an unbearable sadness come over me. "Why must you die?" I said. "Father decides these things. It is probably my reward for coming here safely and meeting you," he said. "But I was going to take you to meet a real cowboy," I said. "Let's pretend you are my cowboy," he said.

THE LAND OF THE VAPORS

A rocket landed in a farmer's field just outside of town.
It didn't explode or anything, just stuck straight down in a
cow pasture. Word got out right away and a crowd started to
gather. Shortly after that the state police arrived and forced
everyone back to a safe distance. The farmer made sure all
his cows were in the barn. Then several army trucks arrived
and sent in several experts to look at the rocket. They were
covered in all manner of protective gear. The rest of the soldiers
assisted in keeping the crowd at a safe distance. I spotted Kim
and walked up to her. "This is quite embarrassing, isn't it?"
I said. "I'm not sure I want these people protecting us," she
said. "This isn't the first time this has happened around here,"
I said. "I know. There was that schoolhouse a couple of years
ago," she said. One of the soldiers turned around. "I wish
you wouldn't be so hard on us. We're still trying to get used
to the new system," he said. He looked so sad I almost forgave
him. "Well, couldn't you experiment with it out in the desert
or something," I said. "They did. They said everything was working
fine," he said. "Well, one of these days you're going to blow up
our whole little town and everybody in it. Do you really think
that's okay?" I said. "No, sir, I don't," he said. "It's not his
fault," Kim said to me. "I know, I know," I said. Just then
there was a tremendous explosion. Most of the crowd, including

the soldiers and policemen, had been knocked to the ground, some of them bleeding. Some injured quite badly. The two soldiers who had been working on the rocket had vaporized, not a trace of them. And the barn had been flattened, a few of the cows still standing. The farmer ran to the barn and started caressing his decimated herd. I helped Kim to her feet. She had a cut above her left eye. The soldier who we'd been talking to was unconscious or possibly dead. I felt his pulse. He was still alive. "He'll be all right soon, I think," I said to Kim. I gave her my handkerchief. "Here, hold this over your eye." We started to walk among the others. "The ambulances will be here soon," I kept saying over and over to those who needed help. I knelt down to one old lady and helped her find her rosary. She thanked me and smiled. I gave sips of water to a young boy with parched lips. Finally, the ambulances did arrive and started carting away the wounded. One police officer said to me, "They train us for this kind of thing, but it never does any good. A goddamned field of cows, who could have expected that." "Yeah, that farmer lost half his herd and his barn, nobody's going to care about that," I said. "I wasn't thinking about that. I was thinking about what a waste of a good missile," he said. Kim and I drove back to town. "Do you want me to take you to the hospital so you can get that eye stitched up?" I said. "No, I'll be all right," she said. "I'm not going to go chasing missiles again. That was a mistake," I said. "Oh, don't say that, Brad. You know it's the most exciting thing that ever happens around here. If it weren't for the army this would be a very dull little town. As it is, it's almost as if we were at war, but with ourselves, which puts a whole other spin on things. You don't really have to hate anybody, which is a big relief," she said. "But what about those two men who were vaporized?" I said. "That was their calling. They went happily to the land of the vapors," she said.

THE OLD SOLDIERS

When I came out of my study, Ginny was standing there with wet hair. "Are you going to town today?" she asked me. "I wasn't planning on it," I said. "Oh, never mind," she said. "What is it?" I said. "I need some stuff for my allergies, but I can get them tomorrow," she said. "No, I can go. It's no big deal. Just make me a list," I said. Ginny had to be at a planning session for the League of Women Voters. I went back to my study to line up several dozen lead soldiers on my desk. They were expensive antique specimens I had saved since childhood. When I had them all lined up the way I wanted them, I knocked them all down. Ginny shouted, "Are you all right?" "It's nothing, just a small accident," I shouted back. She said good-bye and left me the list on the counter. I made myself a bologna sandwich and sat staring at the list. It all sounded like stuff that could kill you. But if it could also stop your nose from dripping and your eyes from running, then good. I walked back and stood at the door to my study: all dead. Then I put on my jacket and drove into town, which was crowded and bustling for some reason. I found my secret parking space in back of the deli. In the drugstore I roamed the aisles until I found the section devoted to allergies. There seemed to be hundreds of products making great claims, all with dire warnings, dizziness, fainting, nausea, etc. I felt myself getting sick just standing there. Finally, I found everything Ginny needed. It was really quite expensive. It wiped out all the cash

I had. When I stepped outside, I saw a mob had gathered in the park.
I asked a woman standing next to me, "What's going on?" "They're
protesting," she said. "Protesting what?" I said. "Just protesting.
You don't need to have a special cause anymore. In fact that's now
thought to be kind of quaint and old-fashioned. I do think it's an
improvement, don't you?" she said. "I always miss the old ways, until
they come back to haunt you," I said. She moved away from me, as if
from a bad aroma. The police were moving in on the mob, nightsticks
at the ready. I heard one of them say, "What is this about?" The other
one answered, "Spoiled brats don't know what to do with their Saturdays."
Finally I made it to my car behind the deli and it had a ticket on
it. This made me sad. There had been a flaw in my otherwise perfect
mission. I drove home and lined up the medicines on the counter.
I hoped Ginny wouldn't faint and throw up, fall down the steps and
crack her head open. I walked into my study and the first thing
I noticed was that all the soldiers were standing up. I was
certain I had knocked them down. Ginny had left the house. No
one was here but me. I didn't like thinking of the possibilities.
Nonetheless, I walked from room to room, slowly, quietly, glancing
at every item carefully. Everything seemed to be normal, undisturbed,
leaving only the uprighted soldiers unexplained. I could just be
losing my mind. That was a simple explanation. Yes, that was it.
Unless the soldiers righted themselves. They are old and have experienced

thousands of battles. Maybe they've learned a thing or two. I
entered my study and sat down at my desk. With a sweeping gesture
I knocked them all against the wall, breaking several bayonets
and a leg or two. I sat there solemnly contemplating my deed.
Ginny wouldn't be home for three hours. That seemed like a very
long time. I went into the living room and waited for them to regroup.
I had a feeling this was going to be a fight to the death, but, still,
I was surprisingly calm.

The thing they're trying to pin on me I simply didn't do.
I may have done some other things, but that one I didn't have
anything to do with. Oh, they'll mount some evidence, and it
will no doubt look quite convincing, but there won't be an ounce
of truth in it. They are masters of illusion. They can make
you believe anything is real. They can make you believe a pig
is a very fine stallion, and you'd be riding him into the sunset
proudly. They said I had plans to blow up a building. I don't
know the first thing about explosives. And I have never had the
slightest desire to blow up anything. They just made this up,
or they confused me with somebody else. But now they won't back
down and are determined to prove their case. My lawyer says there
is no use fighting it, they always win. He advised me to plead
guilty and plead for leniency. I said, "But I'm not guilty. There's
been a mistake. They got the wrong man." He said, "If you plead
guilty, you'll get off with ten years. If you don't, you'll get
life. It's your choice." I would die in prison in a week. I
consulted another lawyer. He said maybe he could get me off with
seven years providing I could prove my amateur status as a bomb
maker. I said, "But I don't know the first thing about making
bombs." "That's good," he said, "then I think you might be able
to convince them." I went home. My house had been searched for
the third time. All drawers were emptied out onto the floor.

Everything was a mess. My private notebooks were confiscated. I already felt like I had been beaten and tortured. I sat there and cried for a good long time. Later that night, there was a knock on the door. There was a heavy man in a dark gray suit standing there. "Are you Ivan Lowe?" he said. "Yes. Who are you?" I said. "Can I come in? I'll explain," he said. I felt like I had no choice, so I let him in. He took a seat and brushed his trousers. "I'm afraid there's been a terrible mistake. Oh, make no mistake, we could make our case, but I just wouldn't feel right about it. I read your notebooks and I was touched by them. You have such a sensitive appreciation of flowers and birds, and your efforts at understanding your friends seem to me quite admirable. You just don't fit the profile of the man we're looking for. Unfortunately, there's nothing we can do to compensate you for the trouble and expense we've caused you. I'm sure you'll understand, we can't very well admit we were wrong. It just wouldn't do. So I'm here unofficially to encourage you to forget this whole misunderstanding, okay?" he said. There seemed to be a great deal of pain in his expressions. "Excuse me, I didn't get your name," I said. "As I said, I'm here unofficially," he said. "Can I get you a drink or some tea?" I said. "Water would be nice, thank you," he said. When I had settled across from him, I felt a great calm take hold of me. He drank the whole glass of water and refused to look at me. "Remarkably fine weather we've been having, wouldn't you say?" I said. "Oh yes, very fine," he said. "The goldfinches have got all their color back, have you noticed?" I said. "You said something about that in your notebook," he said. "Do you like your job?" I asked. He looked at me and said, "Why are you doing this to me? Don't you think I've suffered enough?" "Your pain is your only hope," I said. "I know, I know," he said, and held his arms out towards me.

THE THINKING CAP

I read in the paper today that almost half the nation
is on antidepressants. What a bunch of pussies. I mean,
I know we're living in hard times, but it doesn't do you any
good to go floating off in a cloud. I want to have my wits
about me to know what's going on. Maybe nothing's going on,
just mass hysteria, waves of it sweeping over the country, people
whispering, then screaming, something is invading their lives,
stripping them of everything, covering them with spiders. The
fear grows and crushes them. They barely have the strength to
visit their doctors, who give them pills that make them happy.
And then they become addicted to these pills, and are terrified
of running out or being cut off. Many of my friends are among
these people. They are probably the happiest people I know.
I went to the Think Tank today, although I wasn't sure I could
think. Still, I went. Heidi, the secretary, was there. "What's
the topic today?" I said. "World Peace," she said. "That's a
mighty tall order," I said. "I don't know if I'm up to it."
"You're one of the very best thinkers we have, Mr. Harper. I'm
sure you'll do just fine," she said. I went into my room and
put on my thinking cap. No, I'm just kidding about the thinking
cap. It's a very small room, very spare, no distractions, just
a chair and a desk and a lamp. A couple of hours went by. I went
out to get a bottle of water. Heidi pretended to be busy with
some files. "How's it going, Mr. Harper?" she said. "Love is
all there is," I said. "What's that?" she said. "An old Beatles

song," I said. "Oh, yes, of course," she said. She must have thought I was making a pass at her, but I was thinking of the thorny World Peace issue, upon which I was supposed to be meditating. I went back in my room and took a drink of water. I started doodling on my pad of paper. Soon it was a thick jungle full of animals with men peering out from behind trees. A large python dangled down as if about to attack one of the men. Then a native fired a poison dart at the python and hit it. I don't know how much time I spent drawing all of this, but when I finished I stood up and left the room. Heidi said, "I'm going to close up after you, Mr. Harper." "This World Peace stuff is a load of crap," I said. "Men are killing each other all over the globe. That's what they do. They hate each other over land, religion, money, whatever. It's a way of life. What are we supposed to do, take that away from them?" "Gosh, I don't know, Mr. Harper. World Peace just sounded like such a noble topic," she said. "Tell me something, Heidi. Do you know if Mr. Toomey is on one of those antidepressants?" I said. "Well, I don't think I'm supposed to tell, and please don't let him know I told you, but he started taking Prozac about three months ago. He's been much easier to work for, I'll tell you that. It's definitely helped him a lot," she said. "Well, don't tell him what I said about World Peace," I said. "Good night." I knew I couldn't work there anymore. It made me a little sad, but that's all. I wasn't depressed. A Happy Think Tank just wasn't my style.

PANDA FEVER

I've heard a great deal about the new mall, but I haven't
actually been there. It is full of palm trees and fountains. It
even has a waterfall. And there's a bamboo forest with real pandas
in it. There are wandering musicians who stroll among the shoppers
playing the most seductive music. And the restaurants serve every
kind of delicacy from around the world. The shops abound with the
most alluring clothes and jewelry. The new mall certainly has
people talking, but, then again, I don't know anyone who's actually
been to it. It's been reported that people have gone there and
never been seen again. I don't know if that's to be believed.
Others have gone there and returned home blind and mute. I guess you
could say it has a powerful effect on people. I just haven't had
the time to go there and see for myself. Chester dropped by the
other day and I asked him if he'd been to the new mall. "What mall?"
he said. "There isn't any new mall. That's just a high-class whore-
house." "You mean they're running girls out there?" I said. "This
isn't that kind of whorehouse. This one's running pandas. People
can't get enough of them. Panda fever's breaking out all over town,"
he said. "I think I'm allergic to pandas," I said. "Everyone is.
They just don't know it, and they end up blind and shaking with a
high fever. They ought to run those criminals out of town and burn
that place to the ground," he said. "You certainly seem to have
strong feelings about it," I said. "Well, of course I do. I've lived
here all my life. That damned mall is causing all the little shops
to close. Some of my kin and some of my good friends own those shops.

It isn't right and you know it," he said. I had gotten Chester into quite a huff. I got him some iced tea and changed the subject. "How's Tweetee?" I said. Tweetee is Chester's canary. "You're not going to believe this, Jack, but Tweetee has learned to read. When he's out of his cage, he picks up whatever book I have out and slowly turns the pages. I know he's reading because I watch his head move back and forth down one page after another. He's become very quiet and thoughtful. I select the books very carefully for him, ones that will enlarge his mind and give him a lot to think about. He's reading *Moby-Dick* right now," he said. "That's amazing, Chester. I mean, I always thought he was a smart bird, but I had no idea a canary could read. He could be on television or something," I said. "No, let this be our secret, just you and me. I don't want him to get all caught up in that celebrity thing. Just let him read in peace and quiet. He's a serious bird now, and that's how I like it," he said. "Yeah, you're right, I can see your point," I said. When Chester left he was smiling and he shook my hand, which was very unusual for him. Shirley had called earlier when I was out and left a message, so I decided to call her back. "You won't believe what I did," she said. "I went to the new mall." "Oh my god," I said. "It's so amazingly beautiful. It has the greatest shops I've ever seen. I could have spent all my savings and more. I had to exercise such restraint it nearly killed me.

But I did let myself buy this one great dress and two incredible blouses. And I had lunch in this Ethiopian restaurant. It was like a dream it was so delicious. And the pandas, you won't believe how cute they are. Everybody loves them," she said. "Do you feel okay?" I said. "Of course, I've never felt better," she said. "Chester's canary is reading *Moby-Dick*," I said. "What? Anyway, you've got to let me take you there soon," she said. "Sure thing, Shirley," I said. But my mind was on Tweetee and the white whale. Tweetee's relentless pursuit of knowledge had taken him into the darkest and most dangerous waters, and the whale waited patiently with one thing in mind.

When I went out to get a paper, my dog, Spinoza, barked and wagged his tail and moved his head in such a way that I knew he had something to show me. I followed him halfway down the driveway. Just at the edge of the woods lay a dead body facedown in the grass. It was an older male in a suit coat, that's all I could tell. I ran into the house and called the police. A squad car pulled into my driveway two minutes later. An ambulance followed not long after that. They photographed the dead man, first as they found him, then they rolled him over and photographed him again. "Have you ever seen this man before?" one of the officers asked me. "No, I haven't," I said, and immediately began to doubt myself. Perhaps that is only natural given the circumstances. They asked me a few further questions, but I could only claim complete ignorance. The ambulance orderlies removed the body on a stretcher and sped off. The police followed after searching around in the woods awhile. They said I would hear from them. I felt a little as though I were under suspicion. I took Spinoza for a walk as a reward for his diligence. At night I fretted over the whole dilemma. I couldn't get the dead man's face out of my mind. What was he doing walking in the woods next to my house in a suit, and very possibly at night? It made no sense. And did I know him, or perhaps only meet him once? The police came by a week later and asked if the name Sidney Yarborough meant anything to me. I said, "No, it doesn't." "How about Burton Shelkey?" "No, I'm sorry, I've never heard of either name," I said. "How about Colby Phillips?" "I'm sorry, officers, none of these names ring any bells," I said. "Sorry to trouble you, Mr. Chandler. We'll be in touch if anything further turns up," one of them said. Now I was really troubled. Why were they asking me about three names when there was only one dead man? I wrote the names down so I wouldn't forget them: Sidney Yarborough, Burton Shelkey, Colby Phillips. I couldn't be sure I didn't know men by those names, perhaps long ago and then only slightly. Another week passed and I was beginning to try to put the whole incident out of my mind and get on with my life. I didn't hear from the police again. I started seeing Mitzy again, and thought it best to just not mention it. It's strange, though, nothing ever appeared in the papers. I checked it thoroughly every week. Mitzy and I took Spinoza for long walks in the woods on weekends. This was his favorite activity in the world. He could chase squirrels and birds, and who knows what other scents excited him—bears, bobcats, foxes. Of course, it did cross my mind that he might find another body, but that thought was quickly dispelled in favor of the beautiful day. But back home I started having nightmares. Bodies were being found all over my property, some I knew, in fact were good friends, and some were complete strangers, and my guilt or innocence was ambiguous, unknown even by me. I hated this dream. I decided to go down to the police station and ask for some answers. There was an Officer Baxley working the front desk. I said, "My name is Edward Chandler and I live at 117 West Street. On April 6 of this year a dead man was found by me next to my driveway. The police were called and a report was filed. Can you tell me who this dead man was, how he died, and what he was doing next to my driveway?" The officer searched for the file on his computer for some time. Finally, he looked up at me and said, "There is no record of a dead man found at this address on this date." "You must be mistaken. I was there, I saw him," I said. "Sorry," he said, and went back to his work. Maybe he was an important man, I thought, too important to die, or not important enough. They just erase you. Mr. Nobody has left the planet, no trace, no weeping. But Spinoza knows and I know, we were there.

I was listening to Anton Fripps's Second Concerto for Cello and Violin. Layla was knitting on the sofa. "This music transports my soul to heights I have never known," I said. "What, dear?" Layla said. "I said, this music transports my soul . . . Oh, never mind." "Are you leaving soon?" she said. "Fripps was a genius, but, because he was only three feet tall, nobody took him seriously. Oh, I know there was more to it than that. Yes, he was also a scoundrel. He robbed. He may have even killed a few people. But he also suffered greatly. He had nearly every disease known to mankind at that time. And he poured it all into his music. Really, there's nothing quite like it. Magnificent. Just listen," I said. "Did I tell you about Olivia? She and Rosco are moving to Palm Beach. Rosco's retiring. I hate to think of how much money they have. No more fancy lunches for me. My dear, you're crying," she said. "It's the music. This passage here is the saddest thing I've ever heard," I said. "Then you should turn it off. You shouldn't let yourself be tortured like that over a piece of music," she said. "Oh, but I love it. It's the most beautiful music I've ever heard," I said. "Honestly, sometimes I think I don't understand you at all," she said, concentrating on her knitting. "Beethoven secretly thought Fripps was the superior composer. Many of his ideas he stole from Fripps. Scholars deny this to this day.

Fripps's name isn't even mentioned in any of the histories of music. It wasn't his fault he was only three feet tall," I said. "When are you going to the store, dear? I was thinking of making biscuits for dinner. Wouldn't that be nice?" she said. "We haven't had biscuits in a long time," I said. "It's been years. I just seem to have forgotten about them. They're not really any trouble, and they are so good. It's queer how that happens," she said. We sat there without talking for a good long time, Layla, lost in her knitting, and me, aswim in my concerto. It's true, Fripps lived with rats. He fed them and loved them like they were his children. And when he couldn't afford to feed them any longer, they turned on him. Before that unseemly end, however, he said he got many of his best ideas from them. I try not to think about that when I'm listening to his music. Maybe he was joking. I never think about Anton Fripps as having a sense of humor. "Whenever I have lunch with Olivia I come home feeling small and pitiful. I never could say no to anything she asks of me. And her gossip is so cruel I *know* that she must be saying things about me behind my back. It's good she's moving to Palm Beach. Don't you think so, Wayland?" Layla said. "I never did like Olivia or Rosco. They're both such snobs, if you ask me," I said. "She asked me if I would throw a going-away party for them, and I said I would, but now I don't want to, and I don't know what to do,"

she said. The final movement of the concerto was about to end.
I was crying again. I hid my face behind a newspaper. Such raw
emotion and depth of tone, I was in danger of falling to pieces.
"What am I going to do, Wayland?" she said. The concerto was
over. I tried to compose myself, but I was still shaking. "I'll
go get the biscuit mix," I said. "No, what am I going to tell
Olivia about the party?" she said. "Tell her we are living on
an evil star and it would burn the likes of her," I said. She
smiled. "Biscuits," she said. "Biscuits," I said. All the way
to the store Anton Fripps sat beside me and gnawed on my arm.
I could have thrown him out the window, but I didn't. Instead,
I loved the little man, almost to death.

THE ASSASSIN

A man named Palmquist came up to me and said, "You ought to let people know who you really are. It's not fair, all this dancing in circles, pretending one thing and then another. There's a mystery at the heart of it, and people love mysteries, God knows, I'd be the first to admit. But there's a limit to this kind of thing, and you reached that a long time ago. Why not just come clean, and get it over with. How much can it hurt, unless there is something really hideous at the core of it. And maybe there is, and then maybe you're sparing us. But most likely it's a sham, and it's time for it to end. Stop treating us like we're fools, and then most likely we'll forgive you." "Mr. Palmquist," I said, "I have no idea in the world what you are talking about, but you certainly do seem to be a fool. Now, if you'll excuse me, I have some important business to attend to," and I tried to walk past him, but he blocked my way. "Not so easy as that," he said. "I see your game, I know your tricks. Perhaps there's an evil worm inside you that makes you act like this, and you have no control over yourself. That would be sad, but still I can't pity you. You hurt too many people every day by your false actions, and your blatant disregard for civility. My question is, what do you hope to gain by this onerous behavior?" "Mr. Palmquist, I am a simple man. I try to do good. I have never hurt anybody, that is, until now. I'm thinking that breaking your nose would give me great pleasure," I said. "It's that evil worm working its way through your brain. See, I told you so," he said. I grabbed him by the lapels and threw him to the ground. Then I started kicking him and I couldn't stop. A crowd gathered and someone tackled me. Then someone tackled him and I don't know what happened. I may have lost consciousness for a minute or two. When I opened my eyes they were all gone, Mr. Palmquist too. I walked quickly into a bar and ordered a drink. Next to me at the bar was a beautiful lady, well, it was very dark in there and I could barely see, so, there appeared to be a woman of some sort. "Don't get any funny ideas," she said, "because I'm a professional wrestler, and I could beat your brains out in a second." "I just love wrestling. I just came from a match myself. I was the overwhelming winner, but I don't mean to boast. It was just good, clean fun," I said. "I don't fight clean. I'll rip their face off if I have to. You know what I mean," she said. "Oh, certainly, sometimes you have to do that," I said. My eyes were adjusting to the dark. I could see she was really a beast with a skull and crossbones tattooed on one arm and a red devil on the other. "What do you do?" she asked. "I'm an assassin," I said. "Nice," she said. "I guess I'm not supposed to admit it, but you seemed like somebody who could appreciate it," I said. She had turned her back to me and was talking to the bartender about baby strollers. I finished my drink and left.

Outside, I bumped into Joshua. He said, "Having a little midday nip, are we?" "I just needed to get out of the sun. It was beginning to give me a headache," I said. "Well, I have some good news for you. Patty's coming back," he said. "Patty? Well, that's wonderful," I said. I had no idea who he was talking about. "I've got to run," he said, slapping me on the back. "See you later," I said. I started to walk home. Then I remembered Patty Hooper, but she was dead. He couldn't have meant Patty Hooper, or could he? She was the only Patty I knew.

Jared was standing outside the pharmacy counting his money.
Then he walked down the street looking quite satisfied with himself.
I had wanted to talk to him about a little matter, so I followed
him. He stopped to talk to a young woman outside the pizza shop.
She laughed at everything he said. I stopped to look in the window
of a woman's shoe shop. I couldn't imagine anyone wearing those
ridiculous things. When I looked up Jared was gone. Well, I told
myself, it wasn't important. In fact, I couldn't remember what it
was. I looked in the pizza shop just in case. It smelled so good
I decided to get a slice. I placed my order and a complete stranger
came up to me and said, "Hey, I know you from someplace." I said,
"Well, I don't know you." "You're the janitor from the high school,
aren't you? My son was on the basketball team, and I saw you there
all the time," he said. "I'm afraid you're mistaken. While being
a janitor is a fine and noble profession, I'm sorry to say I've
never had the pleasure. I'm a retired astronaut, twenty-seven success-
ful missions. If you'll excuse me, I must eat my pizza," I said.
"Well, fine, but I still say you're a janitor at the high school,"
he said. I carried my pizza into the street to escape that man.
Vendors were selling cheap jewelry and scarves and African statues
of elephants and giraffes. And one man had set up an easel and
would draw your portrait for ten dollars. I stopped and watched him
drawing a little girl. He was terrible. There was no resemblance

whatsoever. I suppressed a strong urge to tell him. Instead, I walked on. I saw Jared licking an ice cream. I caught up with him and said, "Hey, Jared, I thought about what you said the other day, about how organized religion was the source of all bigotry, hatred and violence. I think you're right. It just took me a while to see it." "Oh, Victor, I was just trying to get a rise out of you. I didn't mean anything by it," he said. "But I thought about it a long time," I said. "You should think about something useful, like how to feed the poor and clean up the environment. You should join our group. We're doing great things. I mean, we're small, but we're doing great things," he said, and disappeared into a crowd watching a mime. The mime appeared to be quite good, if that's your kind of thing. Mimes depress me to no end. I didn't believe Jared was feeding the poor and cleaning up the environment. He just talked a good line, whatever sounded good for the moment. I resolved to never believe him again. It was a beautiful day so I walked over to the park and found an empty bench. Over in the corner a pastor in white robes was blessing some animals. One girl held a python. A boy had a goat on a rope. A woman clutched her parrot. The rest were mostly dogs and cats. I couldn't hear what he was saying, but it struck me as incredibly touching. I could have cried, but I wouldn't let myself. Imagine getting your python blessed! So there are pythons in heaven, not many, but a few. That's some

comfort, I guess. Then, the ceremony's over, and everyone looked very happy and shook hands with the pastor, who looked pleased with himself. It seemed practically like a miracle to me. I got up and started walking toward them, then I stopped, turned around and left the park, a rich man, a stranger.

I tell myself that I'm waiting around for some kind of
enlightenment, but nothing really ever happens. I take the
dog for a walk. He chases some squirrels. He looks like he's
going to get into a fight with another dog, but they end up rolling
around in the grass having a great time. I think there must be
a lesson there. Back home, I find I have been selected for jury
duty. I think, but I'm insane, I'm deaf, I'm blind. I'm the last
person they would ever want. I put on a pot of coffee and settle
down in the living room with a magazine. There's a story of an
elderly widow who lives with her six-hundred-pound pig. She says
that pig would protect her against any intruder. She says it has
already scared off three, maiming one of them almost beyond
recognition. She also says it is a very tidy and affectionate pig.
I have to think about this a long time. I pour myself a cup of
coffee. I think that woman is lying about something, though I've
found that most bizarre stories have some truth in them. The phone
rings. It's Maurice. He says, "Rudy, I need to talk to you. It's
a matter of the utmost importance. When would it be convenient for
me to come over?" I say, "Maurice, you didn't even ask me how I
was. Where are your manners, for chrissake?" "Rudy, forgive me,
it's just that this thing can't wait, and I don't think it's right
to discuss it on the phone," he said. "You still didn't ask me
how I was. Oh, well, forget it. You never have been all that polite,"

I said. "Can I come right now," he said. "How about a week from today, say, at noon," I said. "But, Rudy, this is urgent," he said. "Okay, come on over, but this better be good, because you're interrupting my experiments," I said. Fifteen minutes later Maurice was at the door. "What is it?" I said. "Lance is in jail, and they've picked up Alfred and Felix as well," he said. "What are they charged with?" I said. "Suspected terrorist activities," he said. "Well, that's crazy," I said. "I know, but I fear we'll be next," he said. "I've never done anything, well, there was that bottle rocket, but I don't see how that could count," I said. "It doesn't matter. They've got their quota to fill and they're desperate," he said. "What are you going to do?" I said. "Well, I'm thinking about leaving the country. I've got an uncle in Hong Kong who's promised me a job in a bank. He runs the bank. He could probably get you a job, too," he said. "No, thanks. I've read an article about Hong Kong in *National Geographic*. I don't think it's for me, and I can't picture myself as a banker," I said. "It beats a long prison sentence," he said. "I'm sure something will work out for the best," I said. "Well, okay, Rudy, I just thought you should know. You seem quite content here in your bubble, so I won't disturb you any longer," he said. We shook hands and he left. The article also said that the pig could count to ten. I thought about all that Maurice had told me. It's true, we live in restless, unpredictable times, but you still have to go on being a human being with all the hopes and dreams you ever had, or what's the use? I strive for enlightenment, but what is that, really? A peek through the cracks of the castle wall? A carrot is just a carrot, and a man is just a man waiting for the next thing to happen. But a pig that can count to ten is a thing of glory.

CHERUBIC

I took my daughter Kelsey to the train
station. As the train was leaving, we waved
and waved to one another. I never saw her again.
She went on to become the first woman on the moon.
How she got there nobody knew. And she never
came back, as far as I know. And she never wrote
me a letter, she never called. I just hope she's
happy, my moonbeam. Every night I'm at my telescope.
I've seen dinosaurs, snow leopards, flamingos.
I saw a one-eyed dog wagging its tail. I saw a
mail truck. I saw a sailboat, but, of course,
there is no water. I saw a sign for water pointing
to the earth. I saw a sign for hamburgers
pointing to the earth. And I saw a little girl
fall off her tricycle. A poof of atomic tangerine
dust, that's all. I never saw the girl again.
The tumbled tricycle's wheels kept spinning.
Sleep, I said, sleep, little baby.

I was walking by the pond on my way to town. A little boy, maybe seven years old, was standing there by himself just staring into it. On impulse I walked up to him and said, "Shouldn't you be in school?" "What are you, the police?" he said. "Oh, no, I'm just a concerned citizen," I said. "I hate school," he said. "Well, I can sympathize with that. What are you looking at?" I said. "There's a monster in there," he said. "I've swam in there many times and I never had any problem with any monster," I said. "Just because he's a monster doesn't mean he would attack you. I think this is a pretty friendly monster," he said. "Have you seen him today?" I said. "Sure. He came up to look at me. I think he likes me," he said. Just then a dragon-like creature stuck his head out of the water and hissed. I nearly fainted. "I don't think he likes you," he said. "So it would seem," I said. "Listen, young man, I'm late for an appointment. Are you sure you'll be safe here?" "It's the safest place for me, safer than school," he said. "I'm sorry to have disturbed your peace," I said. "Make peace, not war," he said. I laughed and went on my way. I wondered if I should report that monster to the police or the Animal Rescue League, but soon forgot all about it. There was a motley gaggle of people with placards demanding PEACE marching outside the library. I tried to wend my way through them, but one of them stopped me and asked me to sign a petition that they were going to send to our congressman. I said,

"Sure, I'm all for peace," and signed Michael Flood, which is the name of my plumber. I walked away, flashing them the peace sign. I met Lee at the Black Swan. We both ordered coffee. Lee looked troubled. "What's on your mind, Lee?" I said. "Oh, nothing, really. It's just all so bleak out there," he said. "What's bleak? You'll have to be more specific," I said. "All those soldiers dying, for what?" he said. "Yes," I said, "it's a terrible loss. They sign up thinking they're going to learn a trade. Instead, they're blown to bits. But you can't go around all day dwelling on it. It would make you crazy," I said. "I know, but it's there and it haunts me," he said. "Besides all that, how's it going? How's Kelly?" I said. "Kelly's great. She's going to have a show of her paintings at the Lawrence Gallery next month. You'll be getting an invitation to the opening. We both hope you can come," he said. "I wouldn't miss it for anything. I love her work. It's so dark and mysterious," I said. "I know. It frightens me sometimes. I don't know where it comes from. She's so sweet and normal, whatever that means, and then these weird paintings come pouring out of her. It makes me think I don't really know her sometimes," he said. "There's always a dark underbelly to everything. It's best not to think about it," I said. We talked about baseball, and that's when he got really animated and seemed like the old Lee, but I hadn't really been following the season, so I just faked it, and he didn't seem to notice. And then we said good-bye, and I promised to be at the opening. I walked through town and back by the pond. The boy was gone, and, of course, I had to think about that and wonder if he was eaten. I would probably never see him again, and, therefore, would never know for sure. A seven-year-old boy tempting fate like that, he must have had his dark side. I saw the monster with my own two eyes, and he was real, as much as anything's real.

There was mold on the bread and mold on the cheese. The three peaches were rotten. I threw all of it away and just stood there scratching my head. I had had a bad day at the office. Mr. Perry kept following me around, saying, "These figures can't be right," and, "We're behind schedule," and, "What's with the new girl, Danielle? Have you seen her fingernails? She could claw your eyes out. And the way she looks at me, I think she might try." I couldn't concentrate with all that. He was causing me to make mistakes. Then Mr. Donnelly called from Indianapolis and gave Mr. Perry all kinds of hell and, after that, Mr. Perry sat in his office crying. Danielle came over and flirted with me a bit. She certainly is a buxom thing, but I had to get back to my work. After she left, Quentin came over from the adjacent cubicle and said some cruel and inappropriate things about her. I cut him off and defended her. I said she was an intellectual giant compared to some people in the office. He laughed and said something crude. Then Mr. Perry came into my office and said he was going to have a nervous breakdown. I said I thought those had gone out of fashion. He looked hurt and I tried to console him. I told him I thought we needed to restore our sense of humor, a sense of fun in the workplace might increase productivity. He said, "By George, Benjamin, I think you might be onto something." And then he started crying again. He sobbed and wept all over my office. I held him

and hugged him and told him things were going to be all right.
And then I told him to go home. He said he could never abandon
the ship, he would steer the course, we would weather the storm.
I didn't know where this nautical metaphor came from, but
I looked around half expecting to see waves cresting over our
rolling office floors. "Well, then, go lie down in your office. You
have a nice couch there," I said. "Well, maybe for just a minute,"
he said. Danielle came over and asked me if I thought she should
go comfort Mr. Perry. I said, "No, he just needs to rest for a few
minutes." She asked me if things were always so tense in the office.
I lied and said, "Oh, no. Usually it is quite a fun place to work. We're
always joking around." She gave me one of her fetching smiles and
said, "Well, I hope you're right, because I really do like to have fun. I'd
wither up and die without it." By then I was exhausted. I stared
numbly at my computer. Quentin stuck his head in my office and said,
"Maybe old Perry was having a nervous breakdown." "People don't really
have nervous breakdowns anymore. He's just a little tired, needs a little rest.
He'll be fine, don't worry," I said. An hour passed and I didn't see
Mr. Perry. Two hours. I wasn't even pretending to work. I read
an article about trout fishing in Wyoming. Then I fell asleep in my chair.
Danielle woke me with a knock. "Were you sleeping?" she said.
"Oh, no. I was trying to solve a problem. I often do that with my eyes
closed," I said. "You're a man of many fascinating ways. It's five

o'clock. Do you think it would be all right if I went home now?"
she said. "Oh, yes, by all means. I would say it was quitting time
for me, too," I said. "What about your problem? Aren't you going to
solve it?" she said. "It's all solved," I said, smiling at her. She left. I
checked in on Mr. Perry, who was still sleeping, and then I left. There
was some peanut butter in the back of the fridge and some stale
crackers on the counter. I worried about Mr. Perry. I guess you
could even say I loved him. But if he cracks I will most likely be
tapped to lead the ship, I mean, office. One minute I was full of self-
doubt, and the next I was brimming with confidence. I thought, we're
all going to die, slaughtered like doves. I ate the peanut butter
and started laughing. I thought, I'm going to take this ship down
to the bottom of the deep blue sea where we can rest at last, and maybe
have some fun.

THE PACKAGE FOR PETER HAGGERTY

I called headquarters to see if there were any messages
for me. There was one. It was from Jack. He said, "I think
you should get out of town now and lie low." Jack was such an
alarmist. He always thought the world was about to end. So I
ignored him and went about my business. I fed my birds. I
watered my plants. I changed a lightbulb in the bathroom. I
had no idea why Jack would say that, but, still, it bothered
me. I had no enemies as far as I knew. In fact, people liked
me. Jack dealt with a lot of seamy people, underworld types,
tough guys and killers. It was a wonder he was still around.
A package arrived. It was addressed to Peter Haggerty. I told
the deliveryman, "I'm not Peter Haggerty, there's no one here
by that name." He said, "I was told to deliver it to this address.
Those were my instructions." I brought it inside and put it on
the counter, but it gave me a creepy feeling. I didn't like this
Peter Haggerty, whoever he was. I swept the floor in the kitchen,
then vacuumed the living room rug. Julius called. He said, "Did
you receive the package for Peter Haggerty?" I said I did. He
said, "Good. You are to take it to 356 Walton Road after nightfall.
Do you understand?" "356 Walton Road after nightfall. Yes, I
understand," I said. But I didn't understand. And I wasn't sure
I wanted to be a part of this thing. What was in the package, and
who were these people? Suddenly I noticed that there were spider-

webs everywhere in the corners of the ceiling. This house needed a good cleaning. I went to work. It was easy and very gratifying. Maybe Jack's warning had something to do with Julius's call. He knew something this time. It was a trap. Nightfall was about two hours away, and what I was going to do then I still didn't know. I sat down and tried to relax, but I was very tense and I couldn't organize my thoughts. I was in over my head, but in what? I looked at a city map; 356 Walton Road was way out in the boonies, no streetlights or anything out there. I didn't think I was up for this. And why me? Why did they pick me? I mean, I'm not connected to any of this. Peter Haggerty doesn't mean anything to me. I was letting this thing tie me in knots. When it was finally dark, I started pacing the floor and kicking the furniture. I couldn't stand it anymore, so I grabbed the package and got into the car. I drove out Prospect Street as far as it goes, then, after much juggling and weaving, I finally got on Walton Road. It was pitch dark and hard to read house numbers. Eventually I did find 356. There was a porch light on what could really be called a shack. I stared at it for a long time, but all I could make out was a little old lady leaving and reentering the living room from time to time. I decided to deliver the package and face whatever my fate was to be. When I knocked on the door, she answered. "Come in, come in," she said to me smiling. "You don't know what good you've done, do you, young man? That's medicine from Canada. It's for my boy. He has multiple sclerosis. He's in the next room watching television. You could poke your head in and say hi to him, but he probably won't notice you. Would you like a cup of tea?" "No thanks. I'd probably best be going. I'm glad to have been of some service to you," I said. Just then a big ugly man in a black leather coat walked out of the kitchen and said, "Give that package to me before I blow both your heads off." The woman said, "I told you to stay put until he was gone," and she drew a pistol out of her apron and aimed it at him. "Would you mind if I leave now?" I said. "Get out of here and don't look back. Forget what you've seen," she said. "I've already forgot," I said, and scrambled out the door and down the steps. Back home, I reflected on the mystery of life, then I forgot it.

When Shelley got back from town she opened up box after box to show me what she had bought—blouses, shoes, pants, boots, hats. It was quite a haul. I was secretly adding up the approximate cost, not too happy about it all, but I didn't let on. Instead, I complimented her on each item. *That will really look beautiful on you. That's very stylish.* She seemed satisfied with my performance. "There was this old man who kept following me around from store to store. He'd sit on a bench and wait for me to leave, and each time he tried to sell me this old piece of cloth that he said came from Jesus's robe. He wasn't drunk or crazy. He said it like he really meant it. I brushed him off the first few times, and then finally I stopped to listen to him. He told me a long story of how it had passed down to him through the generations, and it was surprisingly believable. And after much bad luck, he was finally destitute, and was forced to sell it. He had sat on the benches for days eyeing people, looking for just the right one who would cherish this relic with just the right fervor, and he thought I was that person," Shelley said. She paused and looked at me. "And you bought it?" I said. "Yes, I bought it. What else was I supposed to do?" she said. "Well, I hope you didn't pay more than five dollars for it," I said. "For Jesus's robe? It should be in a cathedral or a museum, don't be crazy. I paid for it with my own personal savings, don't worry.

It's none of your business what I paid for it," she said. "Let me see it," I said. "Okay, but don't touch it," she said. She had it carefully wrapped in its own package. Very delicately she removed layers of tissue paper. In the center of it was a two-and-a-half-inch by two-and-a-half-inch square of dirty linen material. "That's it?" I said. "Well, what did you expect? You can't exactly wash it. So it's been passed around for two thousand years. That doesn't take away from what it is. I can't believe I'm now in the direct line of all those who've protected this cloth all those years. I feel like I'm one of the chosen," she said. "Shelley, they've got people over at the university who could carbon date this thing, and then we'd know whether or not it was a complete fake," I said. She looked at me, stunned. "I'm surprised to hear you say a thing like that, Gary. I guess you take me for some kind of fool, giving all my money away to a complete stranger. I guess you could say that it was an act of faith, that I listened to the man and I looked into his eyes and I believed him. I knew he was telling me the truth. I would have staked my life on it. Now what is this about your carbon dating?" she said. "Nothing, darling, I'm sorry I brought it up," I said. "I'm really very excited to have this in the house. It feels so special." "I wonder if we might have to start acting differently? You know, change our lives," she said. "I don't know if I can do that," I said. But

Shelley did start to change. She wasn't as much fun as before.

She had a faraway look in her eyes, and sometimes she couldn't even

hear me. I felt lonely much of the time, and hated the dirty

little piece of cloth. It sat in a glassed-in case in our

living room. I would sit and stare at it for hours trying to burn

a hole in it. It seemed to be fire resistant.

I remember when lightning struck the Hobarts's stallion.
His name was Lightning, too. He was a beautiful horse and they
were devastated. But, soon, they got another horse and they named
her Peaches. She was struck by lightning within a month, and
they sold the farm and bought themselves a huge recreational
vehicle and hit the road. I got postcards from Florida, Colorado,
California, all over, and then they stopped and I haven't heard
a word since. I've often wondered if the lightning caught up
with them. Brian came over yesterday. He looked depressed.
I didn't know what I was supposed to say, because he wouldn't tell
me anything. Finally, he said, "I always wanted to be a cowboy,
but it doesn't look like it's working out, does it?" "That's
what you're depressed about?" I said. "I'm not joking," he said,
"I really wanted to be a cowboy sleeping under an open sky with
a thousand head of cattle nearby. That's my idea of heaven."
"They're a dying breed," I said. "I know," he said. "Well, you
better get yourself another dream," I said. "I'm sure all my
dreams are the wrong ones," he said. "Don't go getting pathetic
on me," I said. "Then you tell me, Neal, what are your dreams?" he
said. "I don't have any. I'm just right here doing my job, reading
some books, trying to learn a thing or two, enjoying myself as best
I can," I said. "That's good, that's real good. Maybe I should
try the same. I always thought it was important to dream, but my

dreams have always let me down, and I end up just sad," he said.
He left shortly thereafter. I was looking for some mason jars I
had bought at a tag sale about a year ago. The basement was full
of cobwebs. It was dank and musky, like all sorts of animals lived
or at least visited there. I'd stored far too much refuse there
over the years, most of it all but forgotten. There was an alternate
life down there, the one I didn't really want to live, but couldn't
throw away. Boxes upon boxes stacked on one another, ancient
magazines, Halloween masks, broken fishing reels, unwanted silverware,
stuffed parrots, and God knows what useless junk. I ran back up
the stairs vowing to get rid of it all soon. I poured myself a
glass of water and sat down out of breath, mildly horrified.
I thought, the mason jars are gone forever into that nether world.
I thought, there are really two parts to me, the one above and the
one below. One part is okay, and one part is dark and scary.
The phone rang. It was Robin. She said, "I'm really looking forward
to tonight." I froze. I had no idea what she was talking about.
"What time are you going to pick me up? Did you say seven?" Where
were we going? How was I going to find out? "Yeah, seven's good.
Listen, Robin, I have something embarrassing to confess to you. At
the moment, I can't remember exactly what we were going to do," I
said. "Oh, Neal, is there something wrong? We've talked about it
for weeks. I thought it was you who really wanted to see *The Mask*.

And then you wanted to take me to dinner at Antonio's. I feel horrible," she said. "No, Robin, please, I'm really excited. It was just a momentary thing. I'll be there at seven. This is going to be great," I said. "Okay," she said, "I'll see you then." I sat there, numb, not able to move, not wanting to. I had until seven to find the human in me, to teach him to walk and talk, and maybe even to care, though maybe that was asking for too much.

BILLY

Nothing could be better than a Sunday afternoon at the
ballpark. However, since that is not in the range of my activities,
I would not be the one who said that. It is that man over there
in the ball cap and loud Hawaiian shirt. I walk up to him and
say, "That was a contemptible, asinine thing you just said."
He grabs my neck and shouts into my face, "Nothing could be better
than a Sunday afternoon at the ballpark!" "Well, yes," I said.
"That is a most pleasant place to be. You can't beat it for sheer
pleasure." He dropped me to the ground and said, "If you dare to
mock me I'll kick you to the moon." I rolled into a little ball
and whimpered. He walked away, glancing over his shoulder several
times. People gathered around me. "What is that?" somebody said.
"It looks like the wasted husk of a human being," a woman said.
"Somebody should sweep it up," a man said. I unrolled myself and
stood up. "My name's Billy," I said. "I was just resting after
a long day. My job's very demanding." They all walked away with-
out a word. It was still early. All the shops were open. Two
men walked by. One of them said, "Nothing could be better than
a Sunday afternoon at the ballpark." I said, "Somebody else has
already said that." He stopped and looked at me. "Oh, yeah, what
does that make me, a parrot? Do I look like a parrot to you?" he
said. "Maybe a slight resemblance," I said. "You think you're
some kind of comedian, don't you?" he said. He came over and grabbed

me by the neck and lifted me off the ground. "You're hurting me,"
I said. He threw me against the building and I slid to the ground.
The two men walked on, continuing their conversation. I resisted
the urge to curl up into a ball. Instead, I struggled to stand up,
and when I did I brushed myself off and took a couple of steps.
Then I started walking with a real sense of purpose. People stared
at me as if I were a lunatic escaped from lockup, or maybe they
were envious of what I had. I heard that thing said again about
Sunday afternoon at the ballpark, but this time I just ignored it.
I thought there must be a disease going around. I felt sorry for
them. I stopped at the funeral home and watched the pallbearers
carry the casket to the limo. I turned around and started running.
Finally, I found the man who said it. I grabbed his arm and said,
"You've got a disease. It's going to kill you. You have to go
to a doctor right now. Trust me, I know what I'm talking about."
"You're crazy. Let go of my arm," he said. "It's going to eat
your brain up. It's very unpleasant. No more Sundays at the
ballpark for you," I said. He walked away, extremely annoyed.
I stood under a paulownia tree, its panicles of fragrant violet
flowers almost smothering.

I was accused of all kinds of things. My accuser, who said
his name was Rogers, said, "On February 1st around midnight you
were seen walking by the duck pond. What exactly were you doing
there?" "I was home in bed sound asleep. That couldn't have been
me," I said. "But we have photographs of you. What do you say
to that," he said. "I've been told there is someone in town who
resembles me, though I have never seen him," I said. "You even
touched a sleeping duck, and he bit your finger," he said. "That
sounds like one of my dreams. Are you photographing dreams now?"
I said. "If you refuse to cooperate things can get a lot rougher
around here," he said. "On February 6th you were talking to a woman
outside the supermarket. She handed you a package. Can you tell
me what was in it?" "I don't know what was in it. I offered to
mail it for her. I was going to the post office," I said. "You
don't know if it was a bomb or if it contained anthrax?" he said.
"She said it was a present for her nephew," I said. "Highly unlikely.
She was one of our agents. She has since been terminated," he said.
"On February 9th you made a call to a man named Aaron Levin in
Cleveland, Ohio. You said to him that you were going to take matters
in your own hands and see to it that justice prevailed. What did
you mean by that?" "Did I say that? That doesn't sound like some-
thing I would say," I said. "Well, we have it on tape. I can
assure you you did say those words," he said. "It was probably some

kind of joke," I said. "Well, you certainly set some bells off at
the agency. We didn't think it was funny at all. On February 21st
you walked by the police department in town and held up your middle
finger. What did you mean by that?" he said. "I was probably
hoping a bird would land on it," I said. "Oh, come now, you don't
expect me to believe that," he said. "Believe what you like. I
am friends with many of the policemen," I said. "Yes, I know. We
have been looking into that. On March 5th at 2:37 p.m. there was
an explosion in back of the bank. You were seen walking near there
shortly before that. There is much evidence that points your way,"
he said. "Why would I do a thing like that? I have money in that
bank. And, besides, I know nothing about explosives," I said.
"You are a dangerous man, Mr. Laganza, and we know all about you.
You'll get your punishment. It's only a matter of time," he said.
I thanked him and left his office. Outside it was a beautiful day.
I walked three blocks and sat down on a bench in the park. Mr.
Rogers wasn't a bad man. Somebody has to keep track of all the
random stuff we do and say. There's a story line somewhere in
your life. We just don't know what it means. He's trying to
figure it out, so that's an important job. He's like a very
flawed, lowly god, poor man.

Molly said she would follow me to the ends of the earth.
"But I'm not going anywhere," I said. "Okay, then I'll just
sit here with you," she said. "I wish you wouldn't do that. You're
making me nervous," I said. "Why?" she said. "Because I feel
you're expecting something out of me that I just might not have. I don't
know, it's not your fault," I said. "Oh, Henry, you're always
underestimating yourself. You know, you're a very great man.
I wish you knew how great you are," she said. "Would you please
stop talking such horseshit. I have studied great men—FDR,
Babe Ruth, Muhammad Ali—and I am definitely not a great man.
So let's talk about something else. How about the fall of the
Roman Empire?" I said. "Barbarians, 476, what's there to talk about.
They deserved it, brought it on themselves," she said. "Forget
it, I was just kidding. They were lazy. I'm lazy, too. Does
that mean I'm going to be invaded by barbarians? What do you
think, Molly?" I said. "Well, I've noticed a few have moved into
the neighborhood lately," she said. She was moving around the
room, straightening things up. "They seem rather nice for barbarians.
One of them has quite a handsome dog," I said. "Yes, I've noticed.
It's very friendly. Maybe we should invite them over for dinner,"
she said. "Oh, I think that would be going a bit too far. That
would almost be conceding territory," I said. "They really aren't
barbarians. I just said that to play along with you. I met them

at the mailbox the other day. They're a nice couple about our age,"
she said. "Let them settle in for ten years and then we'll see,"
I said. "Oh, Henry, do you have to be like that?" she said.
"Great men are notoriously difficult," I said. "I thought you said
you weren't a great man," she said. "Great men change their minds
a lot," I said. "Henry, would you please stop this. I just want
you to be the ordinary man that I love," she said. "I was just
joking. There's nothing great about me. You don't have to worry
about that," I said. "Oh, Henry, you mean the world to me," she
said. I felt like a little pile of dust in the corner. I should
start swirling around and become a dustdevil. That would really
be something.

PARADISE

After Ashley disappeared from camp, I was put in charge
of gathering the firewood. I didn't mind the job, because
I got to be alone for much of the day and away from the constant
bickering that went on with the others. I came back to dump
my armload and then I would be off again. Each day I had to
go a little farther out and this made it something of an adventure.
There was always some wildlife to scare up, and some odd thing
lost or left behind by hunters. I found combs and canteens and
whiskey bottles and a keychain. And once I found a wallet with
three hundred dollars in it. I didn't tell anyone. The further
I went into the woods the more peaceful I felt. Some days I
didn't really feel like returning to the camp. I couldn't stand
the thought of Raymond getting drunk around the campfire and
singing the same song over and over again, and of Tammy eventually
slamming him on the head with the skillet, all the old routine.
One morning I slipped out of my tent with my sleeping bag before
anyone was awake. I didn't know what I was going to do, but I
had a feeling I wasn't coming back. I walked rapidly for what
must have been a mile, then I let myself slow down. I stopped
to pick a bunch of blackberries which were ripe and delicious.
A doe and two fawns stopped to stare at me, then ran on. By noon
I was further away from the camp than I had ever been. The forest
was denser and covered with vines. I had slowed my pace considerably.

At one point I thought I spotted Ashley up ahead of me, but the shadows were also playing tricks. I was using my machete now to make progress. I imagined a huge snake dropping from the trees and strangling me. I had gotten myself into a very inhospitable situation. It was too far to go back, and I had no idea how long it would continue. I was hoping for a lake or a meadow on the other side of this. I kept slashing my way forward slowly. There was a loud screech somewhere, but I looked around and could see nothing. I was convinced that Ashley was in here somewhere, lost and unable to extricate herself. I yelled her name several times, but nothing came back. A small snake dropped from a tree in front of me, nearly scaring me to death. My arm was tired of hacking, and I stood still and rested. I wasn't going to spend the night in this terrible place. There was no place to lie down or build a fire. When I had rested for several minutes, I started again moving forward. It occurred to me that I was being punished for abandoning my friends, but I quickly banished that thought. Something wonderful was waiting for me if I could only get to it. I hacked and slashed with renewed strength. I saw more daylight. Nothing could stop me now. The air smelled fresh and clean. Finally I broke through the last stand of trees and I was standing on green grass. And there was Ashley standing there, naked. I said, "Thank God you're alive! I'm so glad to

see you, Ashley. But why are you naked?" "Oh, Buddy, I'm glad to see you, too. This is paradise, you'll see. It's everything you've ever dreamed of," she said. I tried not to look at her body. "Well, it was hell to get here, but I guess it was worth it," I said. I looked around. There was a dingy shack at the bottom of the hill. "Who lives there?" I said. "God," she said. "Oh, that's just what I call him. He owns me, and when he sees you he'll own you, too. He's not too bad if you follow all his rules." "No one owns me," I said. "Then he'll kill you," she said. He was already walking up the hill with his shotgun in his hand. He looked real friendly, and I was already starting to like him.

I was in the news store when a man came up to me and said, "Excuse me, but could you recommend a newspaper to me? You look like a man who would know about newspapers." I said, "Well, what kind of newspaper would you like?" "Well, if possible, I would like some good news. Does that kind of paper exist?" he said. "I'm afraid not, pal. Oh, there might be a story or two that could cheer you up, but most of it is pretty bleak stuff. How could you not know about newspapers?" I said. "I always read the racing sheets. I thought they were all that mattered, which was the fastest horse. I thought that's what everybody else was reading," he said. "So you've spent your whole life at the track?" I said. "Not exactly. I didn't know where the track was. I thought they were imaginary horses," he said. "I don't think I follow you," I said. "I just thought that's what people did, they raced imaginary horses in their heads all day. So that's what I did," he said. "Did you like doing that?" I said. "No, I was a chronic loser. I lost everything that I had and then some," he said. "Well, welcome to the human race," I said, hoping to ditch this crazy guy. "What time does it start?" he said excitedly. "Does what start?" I said. "The human race," he said. "That's just an expression," I said. "See, it's little things like that that are always throwing me off. I mean, I like a good race as much as the next guy, but if it's not really a race please don't call

it one, at least when I'm around, because I'm trying very hard
to change right now," he said. "Well, good luck," I said, and
started to walk away. "You're going to leave me here, just like
that. You're going to walk away. You don't even know my name.
Don't you want to know my name?" he said. "Okay, what's your
name?" I said. "I had a horse when I was a young boy. His name
was Pathfinder. That horse was my whole life. I would ride him
all day in the summer. Later, he broke his leg and had to be shot,"
he said. He wiped his eyes and looked lost. It was a bad time
to walk away. "What's your name?" I said. "Pathfinder," he said.
"No, your name," I said. "Oh, Oscar L'Etolie," he said. "Well,
Oscar, it was nice to meet you. I've got to be getting on," I said.
"Put your money on Florizel in the seventh. He's a sure thing,"
he said. "Florizel in the seventh. I'll remember that. Thanks,"
I said. "You think I'm kidding? I know these things. No, don't
trust me. I'm always wrong. I don't know what's wrong with me.
I really want to change my life. I was hoping you would help me,"
he said. "But, Oscar, I've only just met you. Surely you must
have some friends or family," I said. "Now you're just opening
up more wounds. I wouldn't have guessed you were such a hurtful
person. Well, if it gives you pleasure, then go ahead, hurt me,"
he said. "Oscar, I certainly did not intend to hurt you," I said.
"Well, the damage is done. Now what are you going to do?" he said.

"I have to go, Oscar," I said. "That's right, leave me. What do you care?" he said. "I care, Oscar, I do, it's just that there are other things in life that need tending to," I said. "Well, lucky you," he said. "What is that supposed to mean?" I said. "'Other things' sounds so important, and I'm nothing, really. I'm just yesterday's tip sheet wadded up and thrown on the floor," he said. "My name's Keith Hancock, by the way. I think you should buy the *Times* and read it straight through every day. We live in a big, complicated world, and I think it's important that you should try to get some perspective on it," I said. "Then I'll know just who you are, Mr. Hancock. It won't be so easy to hide. Meanwhile, try Candy Spots in the third," he said.

I wish I could say what happened to me, but I can't,
partly because of security reasons, and partly because I
don't know. I was crouched on a little country lane when
my cell phone rang. The voice said, "See that barn and silo
up ahead of you. I want you to check it. Get inside without
being seen, and I'll call you back." So I maneuvered myself
around from tree to tree, sometimes crawling on my belly, some-
times dashing, and finally slipped into the barn. It was dark
and dusty in there. There was a goat in one stall and a mule
in another. There was a tractor and a pile of hay and a bunch
of farming tools. Nothing out of the ordinary. But I kept
looking. I poked around in the haystack. I climbed up on the
rafters. There I found a jug of what I took to be mountain dew.
There was also a big trunk. I was able to jimmy the lock. What
I found inside were a bunch of old hymnals and some railroad stocks
from the last century. I heard the farmer coming so I closed
the trunk and hid behind it. He opened the barn doors, stood
there for a minute, then closed them again. I would hate to
have to kill him. He didn't seem like a terrorist. Just then
my phone rang. "What did you find?" he asked. "A goat, a mule,
a tractor, a haystack and some old hymnals. Oh, and some railroad
stocks from the 1870s," I said. "Bring those with you," he said.
"What?" I said. "The railroad stocks. That's what we were looking

for," he said. So I gathered up the crumbling railroad stocks in an old feedsack and climbed back down and snuck out of the barn. I looked sort of like a hobo walking down the road with that old feedsack thrown over my shoulder, so when the same farmer that I'd robbed stopped to ask me if I wanted a ride into town I said, "Sure." "I take it you're not from around here. I know you're not 'cause I would have seen you before," he said. I said, "I'm from Peoria, Kentucky." "You mean Illinois. Peoria's in Illinois," he said. "There's a Peoria in Kentucky, too. It's just a little bitty town of 200. Nobody's ever heard of it, except it grows the largest oranges in the world. That's our only distinction," I said. "They don't grow oranges in Kentucky. Why would you want to lie to me about something like that? I'm a farmer," he said. "Well, that's what my mama told me as a child. She probably just wanted to give me something to be proud about," I said. "Your mama was a liar, was she? Is that what you're saying?" he said. "My mama was a good Christian woman, it's just that we were poor," I said. His disdain for me was evident, so we just sat in silence the rest of the way. When I thanked him for the ride, he said, "That looks like one of my feedsacks you're carrying." I said, "Oh, no, sir, I've had this since I was a boy." "I suppose your lying mama gave it to you for Christmas." "How'd you know that?" I said. He walked away in disgust. Someone was supposed to pick me up here within an hour, but I didn't know who. I was told to wait by the fountain, but there was no fountain. So I sat on a bench near the center of town. A woman with a dachshund on a leash walked by and looked at me. I said, "Excuse me, but is there a fountain in this town?" "You'd be lucky if you could find a toilet," she said. So I sat and waited, and no one ever came.

LIVERPILL

The monster came back again tonight. He must live
somewhere in this house, because I heard no door or window
open. I'm no longer afraid of him, just repulsed. He's about
three feet tall with little beady eyes and a small mouth
with a few short, dull teeth. He just stood there and stared
at me. I don't know if he wanted food or what, but I tried to
ignore him. I mean, he was an intruder and I could have shot
him. The law would be on my side. But, never having seen a
monster before, I thought he should be preserved for scientific
purposes, if nothing else. But, then, over the course of
several months since his first appearance, I still had failed
to notify the proper authorities. I'm watching television
or reading a book and he just stands there looking at me.
He's a kind of yellowish gray color with clots of fur here and
there, really kind of atrocious to look at. I've given him
a name. I call him Liverpill. I said, "Liverpill, why don't
you go sit down and we'll watch the news together." He belched
and just looked at me. I couldn't tell if he liked me or hated
me. I said, "Liverpill, you are beginning to get on my nerves.
If you are going to live in this house there are certain rules
you are going to have to abide by. You can't just stand there
staring at me. That's rude. Dinner is served at 6:30. And
you must do your share of cleaning up. Some polite conversation
would be appreciated. You can tell me about your day, what
you have accomplished and so on. Do you understand me?" He

took a step toward me and belched. "I am a monster, not a house-
wife. I can eat you any time I want, I'm just not hungry yet,
still digesting my last meal, a family of four. Your time will
come," he said. "So you can speak," I said. "Only when I'm
very angry," he said. Now I was very uneasy, thought I had
better develop some strategies. My hunting rifle was in the
bedroom closet, but this didn't seem the time to try and get it.
"I had no intention of angering you, I just thought if we were
going to be living together we might find a way to make it easier
on both of us," I said. "Life is hard, and it will always be
hard," he said. Of course it would be hard if you were that
ugly. I decided to drop all attempts at conversation. I wasn't
concerned about scientists anymore. I wanted Liverpill
dead. And I couldn't very well count on the police if I called
them and told them I had a monster in my house. So it was
up to me to dispatch this ugly man-eating creature. "Excuse
me, I'm going to lie down for a few minutes. Terribly tired,"
I said. In the bedroom, I found the rifle and loaded it. I
feared this was going to be a terrible mess. I took several
deep breaths, then walked back into the living room, rifle
at the ready. He was standing there looking at me. "I hate
this part," he said. "Me, too," I said. I fired the first
shot and he started walking toward me. I fired again and he
didn't stop. I fired again and he walked right into me.
"Liverpill," I said, "where are you? Where are you hiding?"

I was on my way to Thompsonville when a dead raccoon appeared in the center of the road. I guess I could have swerved and gotten around it, but since there was no traffic I decided to stop and remove it myself. I pulled over to the side and got out. I put on a pair of work gloves. I grabbed it by its tail and dragged it a few feet. I thought I saw one eye blink. I dragged it a few more feet. "You're hurting me," a voice said. I dropped the tail and the creature rolled over and stood on all fours. It shook itself several times, then proceeded to walk away. In the tall grasses by the side of the road six little ones were waiting for it. They jumped on their mother with glee and rolled all over her. She swatted them gently when it got to be too much for her. Then they trailed off single file into the brush. I got back in the car and drove on. I was meeting Dennis for lunch. I had no trouble finding the restaurant because it was right on Main Street. When I went in Dennis stood up to greet me. "It's been a while," he said. "Too long. How've you been?" I said. "Just great. And yourself?" he said. "Well, you know, ever since Ricky went to fight that war I can't sleep. But other than that, I'm okay. I'm getting by," I said. "Well, I can't blame you. I'd be the same if Doug were over there. He's delivering pizzas and staying out all night raising hell," he said. "Have you seen Sophie since you split up?" I said. "Oh, many times. She borrows money from me every week, and she's

worried about Doug," he said. "Are you worried about him?" I said.
"He'll settle down. Hell, you're only young once, might as well
have some fun. Look at us, all we do is work, right?" he said.
"On Sundays I watch a ball game on TV. That's my big idea of fun,"
I said. "How's Brenda holding up?" he said. "She's worried sick
about Ricky, writes him letters every day," I said. "Why are we
there? It makes no sense. God, I wish it were over," he said.
We both fell silent. The waitress delivered our food. "Dennis,
would you believe me if I told you a raccoon spoke to me today?"
I said. Dennis laughed. "What did he say?" he said. "She said,
'You're hurting me,'" I said. "I thought she was dead and I was
pulling her by the tail to the side of the road." "But she wasn't
dead and she spoke to you," he said. "Yes," I said. "Sure, I
believe you, John. Why would you make something like that up?
When I was a little boy we had a pet wolf. We'd raised him as a
pup. His mother had been killed. And I always talked to him,"
he said. "But did he talk to you?" I said. "No, but we could
read each other's thoughts. He didn't need to talk. Everything
that mattered was perfectly clear. He saved my life several times,"
he said. I waited to hear the stories, but he didn't offer any.
After we finished our lunch we went for a walk. Thompsonville
was a pretty little town with many Victorian mansions. "What was
the name of your wolf?" I asked. "Gipsy. But there was one thing

about Gipsy you should know: I just made him up. I mean, I believed I had a wolf named Gipsy, but he was invisible to all people but me. He was very real to me, and I even believed he saved my life, that's how real he was to me," he said. "I believe you," I said. "Whatever happened to him?" "Shortly after my sixteenth birthday he died, old age. I wept and buried him in the backyard. My mother watched me from the kitchen window. She knew," he said. "Yes, mothers always do," I said.

TERMINIX

I sat in my study working on some problems. They are far
beyond my comprehension, so I just move figures around, making
columns look real neat, clipping off loose ends. I have almost
hypnotized myself; in fact, I'm downright drowsy. Why I haven't
been fired I'll never know. Everything about this job baffles
and annoys me. Mr. Haggerty thinks I'm a genius, that I'm somehow
beyond the everyday mundane workings of the business. I let him
think that. Why not? It provides cover for my incomprehension.
Kerry is Mr. Haggerty's private secretary. She's not supposed to
talk to us. But one day I was alone with her in the office and
I said, "Kerry, I don't even know what we're doing here. Surely
you know something. Can you give me a hint?" "We're not supposed
to know, Mr. Seymour. It's all set up so you can do your job
without knowing. You're supposed to enjoy the mystery of it. I know
I do. It's very satisfying to me at the end of the day to know
I've helped out without knowing anything. You have so much less
baggage to carry home with you," she said. "Does it have anything
to do with panda bears?" I said. She laughed. "Not that I know of.
Why do you ask?" she said. "I thought I saw a very large order for
bamboo plants one day and it just entered my mind that some pandas
might be involved. Just grasping for straws I guess," I said. "Frankly,
I always assumed it was something more in the line of missiles," she
said. "I guess it's best not to know. Missiles would just depress

me," I said. "I shouldn't be talking to you, you know. I could get

into an awful lot of trouble," she said. "You're very nice, Kerry.

I promise I won't say a word," I said. After Mr. Haggerty came back,

he came to my office. "What did you and Kerry talk about while I was

gone?" he demanded. "We didn't talk, sir," I said. "Yes, you did.

I could see it on her face. She's no good at lying. What did you

talk about?" he said. "We talked about panda bears, sir," I said.

"Panda bears? Why in the world would you talk about panda bears?"

he said. "Well, I'm very fond of them and I asked her if she was, too.

That's all, sir. Very innocent, as you can see," I said. "I'm not

so sure about that. I suspect you've broken a code and it could cost

us millions of dollars, not that you're not worth it, but I advise

you to stop snooping around if you know what's good for yourself,"

he said, and left my office. I didn't know anything about codes or

breaking codes. I took a briefcaseful of files home that night. I

moved figures around, straightened out columns until slowly it was beginning

to dawn on me that we were in charge of the whole world, who would die

and who would live, who would move here and who would move there, who

would starve and who would have plenty to eat, and which wars would

be fought and who would win. I felt sick, nauseous, and I threw up.

I was cold, shivering, so I crawled in bed and pulled the covers up.

I fell asleep and dreamed I was a nematode eating the roots of a

beautiful flower. When I woke I was late. I dressed and rushed to work without shaving or bathing. Mr. Haggerty came into my office shortly after I arrived. "Looks like you had a rough night. Out with the boys, no doubt. Well, I just wanted to straighten you out on one thing: the panda isn't a bear at all. It's a member of the raccoon family. Isn't that a kicker? Oh, and I realized you didn't crack any codes, so you're not going to cost us any money. Our operation will go on as before, completely in the dark, run by helpless innocents, doing our good deeds for the public weal," he said. "But I know everything," I said. "Impossible! There is nothing to know," he said.

THE ROSARY

I had just returned from a trip and was sorting through
my mail. It was mostly bills and advertisements. There were
three letters from my congressman wanting donations. There was
a postcard from Spain from somebody called Butch saying he was
having a terrific time. I don't know any Butch. There was a
fake check for $3,500 from a car company. I opened a manila
envelope and a blue-beaded rosary fell out with a scrap of paper.
On the paper was written in tiny, perfect handwriting, "This
must be yours. I found it in my panties this morning, L."
I'm not even Catholic, and I don't know who L. is. Still, the idea
that this rosary had been in her panties was not exactly displeasing.
I put the rosary on the mantel along with all my other sacred
objects. It was good to be home and see my plants had survived.
I lugged my suitcase into the bedroom and began to unpack. So much
dirty laundry, but also some pawpaws, a slab of petrified wood and
a rubber snake. The snake is a giant blacksnake. I only bought it
because it looks so real, like the one we had in the shed when I
was a child. I always liked that snake, because it never moved.
Then I went about watering my plants. The house was creaking and
groaning. Sometimes I thought I could hear it breathing, almost
wheezing, like it had smoked too much. It was probably a little
sick, but what could I do about it? After I finished watering I
went into the living room and sat down in my big easy chair. I picked
up the phone and dialed Tracy. "Hi, I'm back," I said. "The trip
was a success. I got everything I wanted. How are you?" "Well,

I heard something strange the other day. I don't even know that I should tell you. You know that new girl Linda that works at the malt shop? She said you left a crucifix in her panties," she said. "It wasn't a crucifix. It was a rosary," I said. "Oh, so you did do it. I just couldn't believe it," she said. "No, I didn't do it. Somebody sent me a rosary in the mail and said they found it in their panties. I guess it was this Linda girl, who I don't even know," I said. "Then why did she think it was you?" she said. "Maybe she had a one-night stand and the guy didn't want to use his own name, so he gave her mine. I don't know, but I swear I don't even know this girl," I said. "Anyway, I think she's a little twisted. Paul's in some kind of crisis, but he won't talk about it. I invited him over for dinner Thursday night, but he declined. Maybe you can talk to him and see if there's anything we can do to help. It makes me sad to see him like this," she said. "I'll see what I can do, but you know Paul. He's so damned private," I said. "Evan and Gail are getting divorced. Did you know that?" she said. "I suspected it. They haven't been getting along for years. It's probably for the best for both of them," I said. "You're so wise," she said. "You're mocking me," I said. "I wouldn't dream of it," she said. "Good night, Tracy," I said. I walked over to the mantel and held up the rosary. It looked very old. I wondered how many prayers had been said with it, and if any of them had been answered, but I guess it is the faith that matters most, only to end up in Linda's panties.

THE MARCH

There were two or three stragglers who couldn't keep up
with the rest. I said to the captain, "What should we do about
the stragglers?" He said, "Shoot them. Stragglers are often
captured by the enemy and tortured until they reveal our where-
abouts. It is best to not leave them behind." I went back to
the stragglers and told them that my orders were to shoot them.
They started running to catch up with the rest. Then a sniper
was shot out of a tree. "Good work," said the captain. Then
we climbed a mountain. Once we were on top, the captain said,
"I'll give a hundred dollars to anyone who can spot the enemy."
Nobody could. "We'll spend the night here," the captain said.
I was appointed first lookout. I smoked a cigarette and looked
into the forest below through my night-vision glasses. Something
moved, but it was hard to tell what it was. There was a lot of
movement, but it didn't seem like men, more like animals. I soon
fell asleep. When Juarez tapped me on the shoulder to tell me he
would take over, he said, "You were asleep, weren't you?" I
stared at him with pleading eyes. "The captain would have you
shot, you know?" I didn't say anything. The next morning Juarez
was missing. "Captain, do you want me to send out a search party?"
I said. "No, I always suspected he was with the enemy," he said.
"Today, we will descend the mountain." "Yes, sir, captain," I
said. The men tumbled and rolled, bounced up against trees and

"That man is a monster," Ruby said. "We have to get you out of
here." She helped me out of bed and led me to the door. "You
have to get back up on your donkey," she said. "He will lead you
to a safer spot. Go now, before you're discovered," she said.
I thanked her for her help. The donkey walked on and on, late
into the night, though I couldn't see a thing. I imagined swaying
palm trees and dancing girls, though I knew there was nothing
like that. Probably just some old oil barrels and some empty
boxes of fruit, and I remembered a toy sailboat crashed on a
rock somewhere, still struggling to be free. And I saw an old
man standing beside us shaking his hands and nothing coming out
of his mouth. Something deep down was broken.

THE WAR NEXT DOOR

I thought I saw some victims of the last war bandaged and
limping through the forest beside my house. I thought I recognized
some of them, but I wasn't sure. It was kind of a hazy dream
from which I tried to wake myself, but they were still there,
bloody, some of them on crutches, some lacking limbs. This sad
parade went on for hours. I couldn't leave the window. Finally,
I opened the door. "Where are you going?" I shouted. "We're
just trying to escape," one of them shouted back. "But the war's
over," I said. "No it's not," one said. All the news reports had
said it had been over for days. I didn't know who to trust. It's
best to just ignore them, I told myself. They'll go away. So I
went into the living room and picked up a magazine. There was a
picture of a dead man. He had just passed my house. And another
dead man I recognized. I ran back in the kitchen and looked out.
A group of them were headed my way. I opened the door. "Why
didn't you fight with us?" they said. "I didn't know who the
enemy was, honest, I didn't," I said. "That's a fine answer. I
never did figure it out myself," one of them said. The others looked
at him as if he were crazy. "The other side was the enemy, obviously,
the ones with the beady eyes," said another. "They were mean,"
another said, "terrible." "One was very kind to me, cradled me
in his arms," said one. "Well, you're all dead now. A lot of
good that will do you," I said. "We're just gaining our strength

back," one of them said. I shut the door and went back in the living room. I heard scratches at the window at first, but then they faded off. I heard a bugle in the distance, then the roar of a cannon. I still didn't know which side I was on.